WILLIS WILBUR

Wows the World

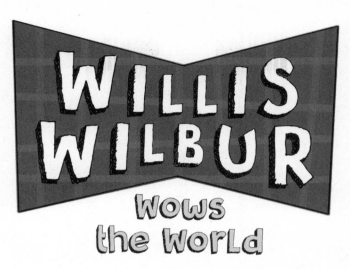

by Lindsey Leavitt
illustrated by Daniel Duncan

PENGUIN WORKSHOP

To James, for your eternal enterprise and enthusiasm.
You're basically Willis Wilbur, forty years later.

PENGUIN WORKSHOP
An Imprint of Penguin Random House LLC, New York

Text copyright © 2022 by Lindsey Leavitt, LLC.
Illustrations copyright © 2022 by Daniel Duncan. All rights reserved.
Published by Penguin Workshop, an imprint of Penguin Random House LLC, New York.
PENGUIN is a registered trademark and PENGUIN WORKSHOP is a trademark of
Penguin Books Ltd, and the W colophon is a registered trademark of
Penguin Random House LLC.
Printed in the USA.

Visit us online at www.penguinrandomhouse.com.

Library of Congress Cataloging-in-Publication Data is available upon request.

ISBN 9780593224052   10 9 8 7 6 5 4 3 2 1 LSCC

CHAPTER 1

The Yearbook Signing Party!

Finishing third grade was a big deal. Though maybe *finishing* isn't a strong enough word. *Accomplishing? Conquering.* That's it. Third grade was the end of the middle. Third grade was finally being old enough to play four square, but never making it to the A square. Third grade was moving into bigger fractions and science experiments. There was nothing *little* about third grade.

But fourth grade? Fourth grade would be difficult division and long book reports. Important secrets.

Maybe some of us would start wearing deodorant. We would be "upperclassmen." Not only would I be older than many of the kids at Green Slope Elementary, but also taller. Wiser. Fourth grade was a responsibility I was thrilled to accept.

On the last day of third grade, I gave Mrs. Harding a "Teachers Are Tubular!" mug before heading into the cafeteria for the yearbook signing party. My best friend, Shelley Kalani, was in the office, talking to her mom.

Mrs. Kalani was the school nurse, which was a busy job during the last days of school. Too many kids throwing books or tripping as they ran in circles screaming "Summer!"

In a few more days Shelley and I would be leaving for six whole weeks of summer band camp. So, when I wasn't signing yearbooks, I was adding to my list of extra stuff I still needed to pack. Things you might forget, like a water bottle or an essential oil diffuser.

I hoped Shelley would hurry, so I could use her gel pen collection. In the meantime I had to sign everyone's yearbooks with a regular blue pen, which is just as embarrassing as it sounds. My name just looks better in teal. On the plus side I'd worked on my *cursive* signature all night. My wrist was sore, but at least I'd come up with the perfect phrase to write in everyone's book.

Here, look:

~~Hope~~ you have a busy summer. Go make something of yourself!

    Best,

    Willis Wilbur

PS Call me sometime. We'll catch up: 970-555-0139.

I bet when my name comes up months from now, kids would say, *Willis Wilbur? The guy with the clever yearbook advice?*

Finally, Shelley ran through the cafeteria doors. I should tell you—Shelley doesn't just spontaneously run, not unless she's on the softball field. She's far more collected than that. Have you ever heard the saying "Calm as a clam"? That's Shelley. (Except I say "calm as a shell," since Shell is her nickname. We always laugh at that one.)

"Willis! Willis! You're not going to believe it." Shelley slid into a seat next to me. I held up my hand to show that

4

I had to finish with this autograph, but once I was done, she had my full attention.

"You got four new gel pen colors?" I asked.

"What?" Her face fell. "Oh yeah. I forgot to get those."

Ugh, my little blue pen just got sadder. Maybe I could trade Caleb Ito some gum for his red pen.

"Listen to what happened." Shelley grabbed my arm. "My mom! Got a job!" She continued to talk really fast, but all I could catch were words like *summer nurse* and *Hawaii*.

"Hawaii?" I repeated. I knew that Shelley moved here from Hawaii in kindergarten. But in that moment I kind of forgot where Hawaii was. Not that close to Green Slope, Colorado, right? Where's a map when you need it?

"Yes! Mom applied for a job. She's gonna be a nurse at a fancy camp in Oahu. It's close to my aunty's house. There's a place to stay!"

"So you get to visit your mom in Hawaii after we go to band camp?" Maybe they'd invite me to come along, too. Wow, Hawaii! Now I remembered—an archipelago of islands in the Pacific Ocean. Maybe we'd visit a national park or botanical garden and I would use a word like *archipelago* and the guide would be so impressed that he'd say, *Hold on, I have to talk to my manager.* They would come over and offer me a job as Kid Administrator of Hawaii, and I could help other kids traveling there find cool places to visit. Not the ocean, though—I hate swimming—but land stuff like easy hikes and historic sites! People forget there's a lot of cool things on land.

Huh, I'm not sure what I would wear as an official Kid Administrator of Hawaii, but there's still time to mood board—

"Willis!" Shelley waved her hand in my face. "Don't start imagining yourself as president of the Pacific, okay?"

7

"I'm not." Because I wasn't. There's no such thing as president of an *ocean*, anyway.

"Good. Because . . . because *I'm* going to Hawaii. Tomorrow, actually. With my mom. And brothers. We're staying with my cousins. It's been two years. My mom got a last minute deal on the flights. I'm gonna surf and eat musubi to the max. I'll be there for—"

"Okay," I interrupted. "I'll miss you for a week, but—"

"The *whole* summer." She dropped her gaze. "Willis. I . . . I can't go with you to band camp."

CHAPTER 2

Shelley and Me!
Never Mind . . . Just Me!

Someday there would be a documentary of my life where they'd ask me, "Willis Wilbur, can you remember the one shining moment when your epic success truly started?" and I'd look at the camera . . . No, I'd look past the camera, like I was gazing into the actual past. My voice might even get a little croaky with all that remembering. And I'd say, *I believe it was third grade. The yearbook signing party.*

But that was the future, and in the future you can see all the moments, big and small, that made the future happen. Right then, all I could see was the color blue, which might've had something to do with that blue pen I had to use because Shelley forgot her gel pen set. And why did she forget? Because she was ditching me for Hawaii.

"The only reason . . ." My voice was sort of shouty, so I started again. "The only reason I was going to that camp was because you love the clarinet so much! I was going to learn the sousaphone because you said it didn't matter if I knew how to play it already. 'Obscure instruments will get you in.' That's what you told me."

"I know. I'm sorry." Shelley leaned her head onto my shoulder.

"How am I going to do summer without you?" I asked. My voice sounded small, like my heart. But my head felt big, like it was going to explode from a growing headache.

Just then, Margo Clawson stuck her yearbook under

my nose. Anyone could see that Shelley and I were in a serious conversation and no longer signing autographs, but not Margo. That girl was all business.

"Can you please sign on page five, Willis? Shelley already signed my yearbook last night when our families had dinner together. Shells, I just heard the awesome news. Hawaii!"

The girls started chattering while I did my best to stay focused on the page. My pen pressed so hard on the paper that I'm pretty sure the imprint would show up on the next three pages. Margo's dad and Shelley's dad went to college together so they were automatic friends when Shelley moved here. They are not as close as Shelley and me, though. No one is as close as us. Everyone knows that.

And Margo had a lot of nerve asking for my signature. We weren't friends—nowhere near it. Not since the First-Grade Episode, which I don't feel like thinking about. Let's just say, after that incident, it took a really big person to sign her yearbook.

Dear Margo,

I hope you leave town a lot this summer.
Maybe I'll see you in fourth grade but probably not.

Cordially,
Willis Wilbur

Even with the stress and surprise, my signature still looked perfect. I pushed the yearbook back to Margo and stood up to leave. Maybe Mrs. Kalani would let me rest in her office.

"Will I see you at the community pool this summer?" Margo asked me.

"No."

"What about at the rec center?" she asked. "You can come over for lunch. I don't know if you heard, but I almost made it on the *Best Kids Cook* show last year."

"I heard. Everyone heard." I turned to Shelley. "I have to go to the office."

"I'll go with you." Shelley waved at Margo. "Aloha, Margo!"

We walked in silence, finally stopping by the front bulletin board (our school always has amazing front bulletin boards. This one was beach-themed: Sun and Sentences!). Shelley decided this was a good place to finish our life-changing discussion.

"What are ya thinking?" she asked.

"You know I can't handle Margo."

"She's a person, not a bike. She doesn't need handling." Shelley swept her long black hair into a ponytail. "I want you to hang out this summer. Her mom has her doing all these activities for adults—like finance courses. She needs to learn kid stuff."

"I'm not a coach!" I said. "How do I teach something like that?"

"She's my friend. You're my friend. I think you should be friends. For Real."

"There's no way. The First-Grade Episode was only two years ago and it's still very raw."

Shelley rolled her eyes. "Will, I know you don't like talking about it. Maybe she didn't mean it. Or maybe she's sorry. Or maybe she even forgot—"

"Enough." I held up my hand. "Margo is not the

14

problem. I mean, she's *got* a problem, but let's drop it. Back to Hawaii."

"Are you gonna be okay?" Shelley asked. Her eyes sparkled with hope.

The islands were a piece of Shelley's soul. She loved it. Missed it. It's not like I could be mad or even sad about this news. Not right now. If my friend was happy, then I needed to be happy for her happy.

The bell rang. Shouts and kids filled the hall. All the noise swirled around us, but Shelley and I were like the eye of a storm. We always were.

"Totally," I said.

"Your mom can still get her money back on camp," she said. "We can go next year instead, yeah?"

"I'm really excited for you." I swallowed. "Really."

The hallways emptied. We were back to being alone. Together. But only for now. Soon we would be alone across an ocean.

15

"Know what, Willis Wilbur? Something wild might happen this summer. Think about it—playing the sousaphone was never right, ya know? Now . . . now you can make a date with destiny!"

I nodded. "The world is my oyster. No, wait, the world is my shell."

I thumbed through my yearbook as I rode the bus home alone. And I discovered something written in all those sloppy signatures . . .

Willis,
You and Shelley are so funny together—Aja

Willis,
I'm glad I got to know you more this year with Shelley
  Bye! Jared

Will
maybe we can finally hang out
next year dude
Peese, Adrian

Everyone saw me as *Shelley and me*. Not just . . . *me* me. Willis Wilbur. It'd been that way for at least four years, ever since Shelley and I sat together at the rug in kindergarten. We played a game where the teacher asked our favorite colors, and we were the only two left after the teacher said every color she could think of. Naturally, Shelley's favorite color was glitter. Mine was burnt umber, but now I'm more into azure blue. Anyway—that was the beginning of a colorful friendship of adventure and imagination and trust. Shelley and Willis. Shellis. Or Willey. Depending on our mood.

So, there I was, at the end of third grade, with my best friend leaving for paradise while I dumped the sousaphone for some big, surprising, unknown adventure. All by myself.

I got out my school planner and crossed out six weeks of camp. Over the top of that I wrote in bold perfect cursive:

Make a date
with destiny

CHAPTER 3

Finding a Date with Destiny!

That night, I helped Shelley pack. Maybe *helped* was the wrong word. I drank grape juice and worked on a list in the kitchen while *she* packed everything. Then I double-checked that she had the right SPF sunscreen, plus some fun beach accessories like toe rings and a sun hat. Shelley was very random with her packing skills when we first met, so I used to pack for her. But Mrs. Kalani pointed out that if I do everything for Shelley, she wouldn't learn on her own. I maybe didn't understand why we had to "do things on our own" if we were always together. But now we wouldn't be together so . . . anyway, she remembered the sunscreen.

"What's this?" Shelley pointed to my list.

"I'll feel a lot better if we have this started before you leave," I said.

WILLIS + SHELLEY'S SUMMER SURVIVAL PLAN AKA KEEP IN TOUCH PLAN

1. Set up email accounts
2. Schedule video conferences
3. Set individual goals and help each other achieve them:
   a. Willis: make a date with destiny
   b. Shelley: stick to a schedule

Shelley nodded. "Email accounts? That seems . . . old."

"Not old. *Mature*," I said. "I've wanted a real account forever, but my mom never let me. This gives me a good excuse. Plus, it's more professional."

"Who cares about professional?" Shelley asked.

"It certainly doesn't hurt," I said.

"Why did you write this? 'Stick to a schedule'?" Shelley asked.

This was pretty obvious. I'd always been the calendar keeper. I made sure we had activities planned, favorite snacks on hand, the correct attire . . . everything. How was she going to get anything done in Hawaii without me keeping her on task? She would probably swim all day or read her favorite book series over and over. Plus, who would remind her to reapply the sunscreen?

"I didn't know what goal you wanted personally," I said. "I just thought we could both focus on something separate while we're apart. I was thinking . . . It's weird that everyone always thinks of us together. All the time. Which we are, but now that we won't be . . . maybe we will both have some 'me time'? Then when we talk, we can discuss how we're doing with our personal goals."

"You mean if I remember to call," Shelley said. "Since I'm *so* bad at scheduling."

It might sound like she was mad, but she was smiling.

And the fact that she was smiling made me believe that maybe we were going to be okay. That this summer . . . apart . . . was going to work out after all.

Shelley left the next morning. I didn't see her off or anything. It's not like she was moving away forever. She'd be back by the end of the summer. Saying our goodbyes the night before was better, anyway. That, or maybe her parents said that driving with them to the airport at five in the morning, then taking a rideshare back home alone wasn't a smart plan for a nine-year-old.

Besides, there was something that might get in the way of making a date with destiny: my mom's Summer Fun Plan. I called it the "Summer *Dumb* Plan," but don't tell her that. In the past, I always had to sign up for rhyming gymnastics club or equestrian volleyball camp. Or worst of all—day camp.

Mom wanted to meet that afternoon to discuss a plan B, since she'd called and got back the band camp deposit. Now that I was nine and an upperclassman, I needed to show her there were better things I could do with my time than the little kid activities at day camp. There was no destiny at day camp.

I bought a poster board, then rode my scooter home so fast, I'm sure anyone on the sidewalk just saw a streak of streakiness zip by them. The problem with being quick is that my breathing takes a while to catch up. I stopped on a bus bench to gulp in air.

That's really when my date with destiny started.

I noticed a bunch of flyers stuck to the community wall behind the bench. I took one and my hands shook as I read about an exciting opportunity:

23

Business Owners Organization (BOO) Presents:

THE BETTER BUSINESS, BETTER COMMUNITY SCHOLARSHIP

We're looking to give young entrepreneurs a seat at the table!

Do you have an exciting idea?

A smart business?

Gumption?

Then we want to hear from YOU!

ENTRY: How does your business help your community?

REQUIREMENTS: Must be under the age of 18

Must own a business

PRESENTATION: Friday, June 15, 2 p.m.

For more information on presentation requirements,
log on to BusinessOwnersOrganization.com

SCHOLARSHIP: $3,000 cash

I would have to look up *gumption*, but my gut told me I had it. In fact, I bet that's where gumption starts—right in the guts.

"Hey, where's your girlfriend, Walrus?"

I didn't have to look up to know who was talking to me. Ella Yorkstaff, who was there with Spencer Limbaco. They were part of the neighborhood kids who hung out by the pond. This group played a game that wasn't really a game. Games follow rules and are usually fun. This game was called Rude and, well, maybe you can guess how the game went.

"It's Willis," I said. "Not Walrus. And Shelley is not my girlfriend."

"Roll over here, Tubby!" Spencer yelled.

My grandma calls me "stout," which is a deluxe word for *round*. Grandma likes deluxe words, which is fine, except when the regular word is more right. Did these kids even notice my shiny hair or strong

legs or sparkling personality? No. They just saw my stomach.

I stuck the flyer into my pocket. "If you'll excuse me, I need to get home."

"My big brother started a business," Ella said. "He's

going to get that scholarship in a couple of weeks."

My insides fluttered. "Very interesting."

"He's fifteen. You're only nine." Ella said.

I opened my mouth to explain that age is just a number. If she wanted to talk digits, I once visited my cousin in the hospital *four* days in a row. And I had a *hundred twenty* dollars and *eighty-four* cents in my bank account. And my shoe size was already a big kids' *three*. Add that up. I was practically Bigfoot, a very rich Bigfoot who did nice things like hospital visits.

"That BOW thing?" Spencer asked. "Or BOO? Did you know Michael Morales is one of the judges?"

We all looked right at the bench I was next to because Michael Morales's face was on there. Not his actual face—a picture of his face for an advertisement. You see, Michael Morales is a living legend in Green Slope. He sells houses; he's in parades and sometimes on the news. He is so important, no one even draws mustaches

27

on his benches. My little sister, Logan, met him at the skating rink once and *shook his hand*. I was extra jealous of her. Imagine meeting a real-life celebrity!

"Yeah, and I'm helping my brother with his business so I'll probably even get to work with Michael Morales," Ella said.

"But if he's just a judge and you're not the one with a business, how would you work with him?" I asked reasonably.

They ignored me.

"My sister is going to win," Spencer said. "Faye

started a jam company. I bet Michael Morales loves jam."

"Don't be dumb." Ella squinted her eyes. "My brother is going to win."

"You haven't tried Faye's jam!" Spencer shouted.

I scooted away unnoticed. My brain was spinning with possibility.

The big, bright, beautiful truth was this: If I came up with the right business, then this would top band camp, with or without Shelley. In fact, I could become a living legend just like Michael Morales.

One kid would say, *Hey, do you know Willis Wilbur?* and another kid would say, *Of course, he's my best friend,* even though I'd never met the kid before, and the first kid would go, *Wow, I should have been better friends with him when he was in my class, but he was always sharpening pencils for the teacher* [which was true. It's my favorite thing]. *You're so lucky you're best friends.* And the kid who I DON'T EVEN KNOW would nod and keep pretending.

That's what happens when you're a legend.

And when you're a legend, people don't measure you by your age or weight. They measure you by the legendary things you do, like donating tons of money to the city of Green Slope so they build a building in your honor, or at least plant a tree—one with maroon leaves and loads of shade.

Wow. Just that morning the summer stretched before me like one big yawn. Now I had more possible possibilities to add to my Summer Fun/Dumb Plan.

1. Make a date with destiny
2. ~~Have our town renamed after me—like Willisville~~
3. Become mayor of Willisville, or even Green Slope if they have to keep it that way

Getting this all done in a few weeks seemed like a doable deadline.

I just had to get home and sell Mom on the idea.

30

CHAPTER 4

My First Business Meeting!

Mom was in her big office, crunching numbers. That is her actual job—a number cruncher. Other people call it an accountant, but other people are boring. "Hey, Bug. Are you ready to go over the Summer Fun Plan?"

"Hello, Ms. Wilbur." I sat across from her and folded my hands in my lap. Facing your future can be overwhelming. I needed to stay calm. "Would you like to go first, or should I?"

Mom opened her desk drawer and slid a large file across the table. "I held on to these brochures. Hopefully

31

there are still openings this late in the year. Swim team. Robotics or aviation or fashion or mountain biking or baseball. Playing the harp. Pottery . . ."

Ms. Wilbur/Mom said more things, but I stopped listening. It was the same story every summer. Mom really wanted to focus on my "thing," but whatever that was, it didn't seem to exist in a brochure. And she didn't want me on a tablet all day. I needed to "better myself" in some way. And although that's a very good idea, we didn't agree on the things that would make me better.

I pretended to look through the brochures.

Mom stopped talking.

I looked up.

She sighed. "How much did you just hear?"

"About 5 percent?"

"Willis, you have to do *something*. Logan is going to day camp—"

"No thank you."

"I work from home," she said. "I can't take care of you all day. You have to find something to do during work hours."

"Fear not!" I uncrumpled the BOO flyer and slid it across her desk. "I have a possible idea. I would like to find a way to build my fortune before I reach double digits."

"This sounds important." Mom read through the flyer. "How about we move this meeting into the kitchen. I'll make you a sandwich first."

I mean, I wasn't going to say no to that. Mom's a sandwich wizard. I bet you've never had a sandwich as good as my mom's. The only thing better was my dad's sugar cookies. But don't tell Mom that.

We went to the kitchen. Mom laid out slices of bread and cut up veggies. "What kind of business are you considering?"

This was the hard part. "I don't know yet. Maybe an at-home business? Landscaping?"

"The Finlaysons' daughter is mowing all the neighbors' yards already."

"Oh, I was thinking something like shrubbery art."

"That's fun but . . . there's not a lot of shrubbery here, hon." Mom spread pesto onto a piece of bread. "Let's think about this for a few hours. Tell you what:

34

It's the first day of summer. I'll take you to the pool."

I wasn't a fan of going to the pool. Every time I got out of the water, the swimsuit's elastic waist cut under my stomach, and the fabric suctioned to my thighs. And there was the whole sunburn thing. Not to mention, you don't *go* anywhere in a pool. Just laps or circles. "Swimming doesn't make money."

"Tell that to Michael Phelps," Mom said.

"Who?" But this Michael Phelps guy reminded me of another Michael—Michael Morales—which reminded me I had to make this happen. Not only for the legend thing, but to save me from having to join something else, like the league of soccer puppetry.

Mom slid a tomato and mozzarella sandwich across the table.

"Mom, I just want a seat at the table."

"What table?"

"It talks about it on the flyer. All the tables."

35

A business table was probably very long and metal. The chairs swiveled, and everyone nodded at one another in smart ways, saying things like "Sharp idea, Darius!" or "You're a team player, Sharon." Also, business tables included snacks.

"I get three thousand dollars if I win," I said. "I could probably buy a house or a cruise ship with that much money."

"But we've already missed the signups for a lot of these activities. I can't have you sitting around doing nothing."

PRO TIP #1:
In negotiations, try to give options that are win-win.

"I have two weeks until the presentation," I said. "Let's make a deal. If I win, I can keep working on my business for the rest of the summer. If I don't, then I guess

I'm going to pottery yoga camp." I held out my hand. "Do we have a deal?"

Mom sighed. Mom sighs are not bad things. They usually mean surrender.

CHAPTER 5

My First Idea!

Mom and I discussed the terms of our contracts. I wrote hers and she wrote mine, and we both got to make "revisions."

Our final, signed agreements:

To Whoever Is Reading This (Probably Just Willis and Dad and Maybe Logan If She Gets Nosy),

I, Ashley Wilbur, super promise to let Willis figure out his destiny for a few weeks instead of going to not-fun day camp with his little sister. I also acknowledge that having a best friend move away for the summer is not easy, so I will set up an email account and help Willis stay in touch with Shelley (and maybe drop hints to Shelley's mom about souvenir ideas). I will support Willis by making him delicious sandwiches, driving him to business meetings (once he has them), letting him use my printer for contracts, and . . . whatever else businesspeople need to print. We will discuss Willis's progress as a family after the BOO scholarship announcement. Afterward, I reserve the right to sign him up for yo-yo modern dancing with his approval, but NO DAY CAMP.

Also, I have the best son ever.

Cordially,

Mom

To Whom It May Concern:

I, Willis Wilbur, do solemnly swear to seek out a worthwhile professional endeavor that meets the requirements of the Business Owners Organization scholarship. While creating this business, I will also:

1. Keep my room clean

2. Help with my little sister

3. Practice self-sufficiency

4. Understand that my mother works from home, and barging into her office to use the printer without knocking does not create an ideal work environment

5. Participate in age-appropriate activities, such as bike rides, playdates, and using my imagination

6. Not turn into an adult because I'm still my mom's Willy Bear, even if this statement somehow embarrasses me.

After this self-created course is completed (night of BOO scholarship results), I will reassess the remainder of my summer schedule. This may include day camp, even if I made my mother sign something stating otherwise.

The Best Son Ever,
Willis Wilbur, Esq.

I went out to the garage to get a fruit pop from the freezer to celebrate. My great-great-great-grandfather's rocking chair (okay, we bought it at a garage sale last week) was shoved in the corner. Lightbulb moment!

I poked my head into the laundry room. "Can I fix up that rocking chair?"

"The chair is fine. I'm going to put it on the patio."

"Mom, the chair is not fine and neither is your patio furniture. Everything is the same yucky color, and everyone knows that your outdoor space should match your personality."

"Is this your plan, then?" she asked. "Starting an interior design business?"

Maybe design was my destiny. Maybe I would take pictures of the backyard, and a celebrity would see the photos online and ask to be my client. They'd fly me out to LA, and then just buy my family a house next door so I could decorate houses for all the celebrities. Then I'd get famouser than them, and when they're in an interview for a movie, the interviewer would ask, *Isn't your house decorated by Willis Wilbur? I'm dying to meet him. What's he like?* even though they're there to talk about a movie. And I'd have to apologize, but it would be okay, because friends forgive your famousness.

"I'll get right to work. Don't look outside! I want you to be surprised."

"I'm guessing you want me to pay you for this?" she asked.

"I'll send you my bill."

If I told you everything I did to fix my mom's patio,

it would take me all day because that's how long I worked—all day. I pushed the rocking chairs onto the driveway and painted them a royal blue. I sprayed down the deck chairs. I added throw pillows that the neighbor was going to throw out (get it? *Throw* out?). There was nothing I could do about the ugly coffee table, so I added a bowl of wildflowers on top.

This was when disaster struck. Everything happened fast and in slow motion. The furniture was in the wrong directions. Naturally, I rolled a deck chair to face the sun.

Then I tripped on the new outdoor rug.

My foot got tangled in the polka-dot blanket.

I tried to catch myself on a fern, but ferns aren't good at catching people.

I pulled out a leaf and fell right into that dumb coffee table.

I felt a crunch.

My arm did not like that coffee table.

43

PRO TIP #2:
Decorating is dangerous business.

CHAPTER 6

The Business Article!

Mom rushed me to the emergency clinic down the street. Dad met us there because Mom was on DEADLINE, and let me tell you, a deadline was just as scary as a crunchy arm. Mom's Number Clients got very angry and pointed their fingers at her if she missed her deadlines; at least that's what I think they did. I don't know because my mom was very good at her job.

Dad still had flour all over his nose from the bakery. My dad was a baker and a manager and a baker-manager, which, if you are counting, are three jobs.

45

He paced, hands waving around as he spoke on the phone. My hand, by the way, still really hurt, but it was mostly my wrist. That was the stupidest coffee table in the history of coffee tables, and anyway, no one even drank coffee in my family so why did we have one?

Maybe design wasn't my passion. Of course I was amazing at it, but I was amazing at a lot of things. If I was going to give my whole summer/heart to something, it needed to be special.

Dad muted his phone for a second. "Are you okay? Need anything?"

"No." I wiped a tear with my shirt. "Not really."

Maybe I should wait to retire from design until I fixed this waiting room, with it's boring picture of a sailboat, gross leather couches, and don't even get me started on the glass coffee table. At least the magazines covered up the smudges. I used my good arm to pick up a copy of *Working Parents Weekly*, trying to focus on the words instead of the pain in my arm. It only sorta worked.

But then I found an article that I was destined to find: "Become a Life Coach Using 5 Essential Skills!"

Life coaching? I'd heard about this. Aunt Kaylee went to a life coach when she was deciding what to do

47

when her last kid moved out of the house. She ended up opening a cheese store.

Are you a good listener with a desire to help other people? Have a variety of interests? Looking for a career change? Have you considered life coaching? This growing field is perfect for someone hoping to work from home and enjoy a flexible schedule. Start today!

My heart raced. Maybe I was still in shock from hurting my wrist. Or maybe this was the feeling that happened when your life was about to change . . . forever.

5 ESSENTIAL LIFE COACH SKILLS!

1. Authenticity

This meant being real. I'm real! Realer than real! I mean, really, really, really real.

2. Confidence

Check! There aren't many kids like me in Green

Slope. I'm fine with that. We can't all be legends.

3. Enthusiasm

Enthusiasm for design was part of the reason I'd ended up in this clinic, so yeah. I got that covered. Thanks.

4. Knowledge

Not to brag, but I know a lot. And what I don't know I can learn. It's like they were writing this article just for me. It's like I invented this job myself.

5. A Niche

Who was Niche? Sounds like a French guy. Did you say it like Nick? Did I need to change my name? I would have to look it up after I left the doctor. Oh yeah, I was at the doctor's. I'd almost forgotten about my arm . . .

"Willis Wilbur?" a nurse called. "Come with me."

"Hey, man. I've got to go." Dad hung up the phone and ruffled my hair. "You ready, bud?"

Extra ready! Ready for a wrist brace, of course.

But *really* ready to start a business that would win that scholarship. And after my victory, I would go on my own talk show, where I would fill arenas with lost people who just need the answer, which I would give. In fact,

my work name would be "the Answer Guy." I'd charge eighty thousand million dollars for every answer, except for a few free ones I'd give because it was important to stay humble.

But that was months away. First, I had to get a life coaching business going. Not a problem. I had almost two weeks until the scholarship deadline.

Sweet destiny, here I come.

CHAPTER 7

The Training Session!

To: shelleygirl928@zmail.com
From: williswilburprofessional@zmail.com
Subject: Destiny

Shells!

I have amazing news—I sprained my wrist. (I would have called you, but you were maybe still on the airplane and also the pain made me forget.) Obviously that's not the news. While I was in the doctor's waiting room, I found my destiny. I'm going to be a life coach and win a three-thousand-dollar scholarship and probably make six figures, whatever that means, by September. I'll share my large salary with you. Let's buy matching scooters! I have a lot of work to do, but I wanted to make sure we started our summer emails ASAP.

Your friend,
Willis

To: willswilburprofessional@zmail.com
From: shelleygirl928@zmail.com
Subject: Re: Destiny

Aloha!

Shoots! Your wrist. What happened? Or maybe tell me over the phone. Is typing hard?

Who hired you to be a life coach? It seems like a grown-up job. I dunno a lot about it. But cool. I would love a free scooter. And a glitter helmet.

We got in a few hours ago. Now I'm just unpacking. We are going to the beach with my cousins. The first day coming from the mainland is always sorta weird with ohana. But both my cousin Liliana and I like graphic novels, so we can talk about that.

I don't usually type this much. Email is fun. Good idea. Mahalo!

XO,
Shelley

PS Remember that time we were eating frozen grapes in my backyard? We decided to name every grape. We named fifty and then felt bad eating them. I named the macadamia nuts they gave us on the plane. They're still in my pocket.

The next morning started with a power breakfast outside. Power breakfasts are different from regular breakfasts because they are faster and include more eggs. I read about it in another waiting room magazine. There was also an article on "How to (Comfortably) Dress for Success": "A blue oxford shirt always works, and mix it up with wild trouser colors!" It was hot for these yellow pants, and flies kept swarming around the eggs, but I was a dedicated businessperson now. I wiped my mouth with a fancy napkin and got straight to work.

All the answers I needed were inside my new library book, *The Life Coach Millionaire!* Like, did you know the word *niche* is *not* the name of a French guy? It means "a specialty." And I discovered that there are many different kinds of life coaches out there. Fitness coaches, real estate coaches . . . coaches who help with success, finances, retirement, dating, parenting, business—

Agh! There was too much information. Where was I supposed to start?

Coaching finances to people wasn't a good idea, mostly because I wasn't sure what the word *finances* meant. Or how to help adults with adult problems.

And that's when I had a humongous lightbulb moment! I'm really good at getting these ideas, probably because the initials of my name, Willis Oliver Wilbur, spell the word *WOW*! My parents did that on purpose. Dad said Mom yelled this word the whole time she was delivering me. And I yelled it right then.

"Wow!"

First thing in the morning, and I'd already found my nick . . . my noch . . . my *niche*.

Kid problems. Stuff like bullying and monsters under the bed and starting a new school and tree house design.

Sweaty, stressed adults could go visit adult coaches

in skyscraper buildings with their stuffy offices. My clients could just come right to my house, where I would change the world. Or change my neighborhood, one kid problem at a time.

"Why are you eating out there?" my little sister, Logan, asked. She'd barely turned seven and was smart. Just ask her.

"It's a power breakfast." I picked up my plate with my good arm and headed straight to the kitchen. There were so many things to do! An office to design and a client list to build and a business wardrobe to create. Bow ties and scarves . . . Bow ties and scarves worked so great with this niche. You can *trust* someone in a scarf . . .

"Why didn't you make more eggs for me?" Logan asked.

"I'm on the clock."

"Then turn off the clock," Logan insisted.

"No, it's a business expression." I sighed. "You're

seven. You wouldn't understand."

"Explain it to me while you make me breakfast." Logan bounced from one leg to the other. "Are you starting a new business? Can I join?"

"It's a very small business. Me only." I stared at my sister. She was bouncy, but she did know a lot of kids.

PRO TIP #3:
Most small businesses
grow from word of mouth.

"I'm going to be a life coach," I said. "That means I guide kids with important life decisions. Maybe you can be my—"

"You better not say *secretary*." Logan held up a fist. "I'm more interested in finding you clients."

"How do you know the word *client*?" I asked. Had she read my magazine articles?

"I watch your design shows sometimes." Logan

smiled a secret sort of smile. "Actually, I want to be a consultant—an independent consultant."

I blinked. I had no idea what a consultant was, but I wasn't about to tell Logan that.

"For every client I bring in, you have to give me 25 percent of the profits," Logan said. "And I may become a partner or coach later on."

My sister frightened me a little. A lot. "How do you know about percentages?"

"I don't, really. Or you have to pay me ten dollars. Whichever is more money." Logan hopped off the kitchen barstool. "I'm friends with the kids at the sandbox, my day camp, the kids who ride in the front of the bus, and the Unicorn Club. We're up to six members."

This was tricky math. The truth is, even if I had to give Logan some of the money, that was still more money than the zero I'd have without kids. "It's a deal. I'll email you a contract."

57

Logan scrunched up her face. "I don't have email."

"Oh, maybe you're not mature enough." I sighed. "I'll see if we can get that set up for you. I will need the cell phone more often, you know."

"Yeah, right."

Logan and I shared a flip phone because my parents had Opinions About Technology. Obviously, I would need the phone more for work, at least until I had my own business complex with fifty employees. "Think about it. We can add it to the list of business stuff to discuss."

"You add it. I'm not the secretary, remember?"

My brain was already jumping. Lists happen all the time in business. Like every day. Same with emails and whiteboards. And training. So much to do! Adult life coaches did special training that cost a lot of money and took a lot of time. They earned certificates so they had something deluxe to hang on the wall.

There was also a ticking clock. A deadline—just like

what my mom had. The presentation was in a couple of weeks. So I couldn't do anything too fancy or spectacular. Just halfway spectacular, which didn't seem too hard since there was nothing on the internet about kids as kids coaches. My services were extra *necessary.*

Then I found Clarabelle Coburn, Life Coach to the Stars! Her clients were famous people, more famous than Michael Morales, even. Her website had videos teaching other people how to become life coaches. Advice like:

1. Launch a professional website

2. Find guinea pig client for practice

3. Establish a niche (already done, Clarabelle!)

After I watched her free videos, all 280 minutes of them, I decided I was an expert and made myself a certificate. I just needed a wall to hang it on.

Then, since my art supplies were already out, I made launch party invitations. Now, I don't want to brag because Clarabelle said it's important to stay "grounded," even

when you succeed, but these invitations were *glorious!*
Just look:

 ☆ **YOU'RE INVITED!** ☆

Come celebrate the launch of a new local business,
Willis Wilbur: Neighborhood Life Coach. A life coaching service
FOR kids BY a kid (who is smarter than most adults).
Willis can help you reach your goals and discover your dreams!

WHERE: Willis Wilbur: Neighborhood Life
Coach headquarters
aka the Wilbur family garage,
139 Elm Ave.

WHEN: June 11, 2 p.m.

Come dine on delicious appetizers while you learn more
about this exciting opportunity. Can't make it to the launch?
No problem—you can still call today to book your
first life coaching appointment!

In-person, online, or on-location appointments available.
970-555-0139

Networking was such an important part of building a business that I decided to network immediately. And by network, I meant call Shelley.

She answered on the fifth ring. She sounded very sleepy. "Willis? It's six in the morning. Why ya calling me?"

I forgot about the four-hour time difference between Colorado and Hawaii. I forgot how far away my best friend was during this crucial time in my life. "Sorry. I started the business and I wanted to talk about it."

"That's cool, but can we talk later? Like during the *awake* hours of the day?" Shelley yawned.

"You got it! I'm doing a ton of planning. I have lists and lists and lists."

"Then call Margo." Shelley sounded more awake now. "This is perfect. She loves lists. Have you two hung out yet?"

When would I have had time for that already?

When would I *ever* have time for Margo? "I'll let you sleep. Call me later! Bye!"

I didn't like the feeling of not being able to immediately talk about an important thing with an important friend. And I didn't have time for doubt, not with so much riding on this. But I remembered that Clarabelle also said that if you envision a positive outcome, it would happen. So I did. I imagined myself in my office with lots of certificates and awards and pictures of me with celebrities, hanging on my wall. I imagined a line of kids out the door, kids who really needed to figure out things, and I was the lucky guy to help them do it. I imagined how happy they would be and how happy I would be that they were happy, but also how happy I would be when I, Willis Wilbur, discovered my destiny *all by myself*, and no one would think another person (who I still really liked) did it with me.

I opened my eyes. Enough imagining. Now it was time to DO.

CHAPTER 8

My New (Mandatory) Friend!

By the end of the day, Green Slope was dazzled with invitations. Kids at the grocery store, rec center, dance studio, frozen yogurt shop, and baseball fields would start calling me with all their coaching needs. I even stopped at local adult businesses, in case kids were there waiting with parents. I was hanging an invite outside a chiropractor's office when I saw Margo in the waiting room. Which was good and bad.

Bad because, well, it's Margo. I wasn't prepared. Also—I had no idea what a chiropractor did.

Good because of Shelley. I did not want any of our valuable time spent on Margo. Shelley would ask, *Have you hung out yet?* And now I could say yes, and then we could move on to discussing more important matters, like the color scheme for my launch party.

And Shelley did have a point. When it comes to starting a business, Margo was a useful person to know.

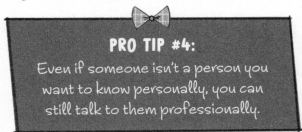

PRO TIP #4:
Even if someone isn't a person you want to know personally, you can still talk to them professionally.

I sat next to Margo in the waiting room, which at least had a relaxing waterfall nearby. "Hello, Margo. I hope you are well."

"I will be after I get adjusted," Margo said. "I carry too much stress in my shoulders."

I still had no idea what a chiropractor did, but I didn't

let on. "I thought that was an adult thing."

"Whatever that means." She smiled. "I was just going to call you today. Shelley said you could use a friend."

"Shelley said *I* needed a friend?" I nearly yelled. Then I took deep breaths, like the professional that I am. "How . . . nice of her."

Margo fished through her purse until she found some ChapStick. "Yeah, she's always saying I need to go 'play' with someone, which is extremely juvenile. That's Shelley for you."

I had to ask myself, *What would Clarabelle Coburn do?* Even if she was uncomfortable and unsure how to talk to someone like Margo. She would network. She would network extra hard. "Shelley's right. Let's do something soon. We can go to the park with the really high swings. Or walk to the ice-cream shop."

"I don't do refined sugar. Hey, what's with all the sparkles?" Margo grabbed the invitation from my hand.

"This is perfect! I would love to be your first client. There are so many things to discuss, like should I go premed or -law? I just don't know."

"Uh . . ." This was also good and bad. Good because I needed clients. Bad because . . . this was Margo.

It's not like I suddenly just forgot about the First-Grade Episode. "You can call the number and book an appointment."

"What about now?"

I looked around the chiropractor's office. This was not the space I pictured for my first client meeting. "My office isn't open now."

"This says you don't have to do visits in your office. We can talk online or meet on location." She leaned in like she was telling a secret. "Okay, I toured some college campuses this spring. I think I want a smaller college, because schools in Green Slope have small class sizes. But the Ivy Leagues are nice, too."

"College?" I asked. "But you're nine."

"Age is just a number," she said.

Whoa. That's what I always said.

Could I work with Margo? Could I see past the horrible thing she did in first grade in order to coach her now? And even if I was a really big person and took her as a client, could I actually help her?

Yes! And as a bonus, maybe she would finally apologize for the Episode.

I did some more deep breathing and thinking. Okay. Okay. College wasn't happening tomorrow, but summer was. All around us. Shelley was right—Margo needed to learn how to be a kid (even though she was wrong about me needing to make more friends). So Margo and I would make an appointment, but a different kind. We would explore how to play like a kid. In a professional way.

"I want you to understand that I coach kids with kid problems," I said. "Not kids with adult problems."

"It's never too early to think about this stuff," she said. "Now tell me, is the party business casual? I'll go with business casual. I bought some nice slacks for campus tours. We're going to California next month to

70

tour Stanford. My mom went to Stanford."

Was Stanford a college? "I actually don't know a lot about colleges. Maybe find a college coach if that's what you want. Again, we would work on teaching you how to be a kid."

Margo just stared at me. I bet she was thinking, *Wow, how does he fit so much knowledge in that head?* Or maybe *How did he see right through my soul?* "You got a haircut. I love it. Your eyes look like emeralds."

I'm sure Clarabelle Coburn would agree that you should not have a crush on your life coach. And anyway, I didn't like Margo that way. I'd never liked any girl that way. "You know my relationship with clients has to stay professional."

Margo laughed. "Just because I noticed your haircut doesn't mean I *like* like you."

"I would be happy to book an appointment with you as long as we can maintain a professional relationship."

There. I did it. I said yes! Shelley would be extra proud. And really . . . I wasn't in the position to turn away clients. When you tell the universe you want something and you get it, it's not like you can say, *Hey, Universe. Can you do better than this?*

"I think we need to start smaller," I said. "Like way smaller. Like . . . maybe we should try hanging out like Shelley said. Meet me at the park on Saturday at ten a.m."

"Are we doing SAT prep?"

"No! Margo, you and I are meeting for a playdate. A *professional* playdate."

Margo wrote our appointment in her planner. Yes, she had an actual paper planner. Thick and official-looking. I made a mental note to buy the same one. Or maybe a slightly better one.

And, just like that, I was open for business.

CHAPTER 9

Building a Client List!

I was feeling good as I walked home that day. Sure, it would've been nice to ride my scooter, but the doctor said I had to give my wrist a rest for a week or so. Then I'd said, "As long as I don't need to give it a break," and my dad gave me a courtesy chuckle, but really, sometimes I'm hilarious.

Sprinkler water flicked my arms and legs. The air smelled like dandelions and manure from the nearby dairy. Such great smells! I loved everything about my neighborhood, which was filled with cheerful blue, white, and yellow houses. My gray scarf fluttered in the summer breeze.

This morning was one of promise. This morning was one of possibility.

This morning was one of . . . poop.

Ugh. I lifted my favorite blue sneaker out of a pile of dog poop. This was not good neighborly behavior. Dog owners were supposed to bag their doggie's business. And speaking of business, who was going to trust a coach with poop all over his shoe?

My house was just on the other side of the pond. Unfortunately, the Rudes were also on the other side of the pond. Well, the Rudes and Adrian James, who hung out with the Rudes, but wasn't rude himself.

"Hey, Walrus! Got any doughnuts?" Ella called.

"What are you up to, Tubby?" Spencer asked.

"Hey, don't do that." Adrian leaned over his bike's handlebars.

At least I had experience if a client wanted to discuss bullying. Dad always told me, I couldn't change their behavior, but I could control my reaction. I clutched my flyers in my good hand and marched over to the Rudes. No one should feel less simply because they weigh more.

"Spencer, good to see you." I thrust an invite toward Ella. "I've started a new business. I think you all may benefit from my services."

"Life coach?" Ella scrunched up her nose. "Are you a therapist or something?"

Adrian looked at the invite. "A coach is different than a therapist."

"You work with crazy people?" Spencer asked.

"No," I said. "And seeing a therapist doesn't make you crazy. Therapists are important, too. I'm more of a guide to inspire you to make positive choices."

Like not wearing neon green shorts with a purple shirt,

Spencer. Which maybe wasn't a nice thought, but it was a factual one.

"You think people are going to pay to get advice from you?" Spencer squinted. I knew this look. Spencer was figuring out his next move in the Rude game.

"I think that's cool." Adrian folded the invite and stuck it into his back pocket.

Hmmm. Adrian was a neighborhood influencer. When he said something, other kids listened. A positive review from him could mean more clients. But it wasn't a good idea to talk business with Spencer and Ella around. Not to mention there was still the poop on my shoe.

"Where's that friend of yours?" Ella asked. "Did you two break up?"

"I told you. Shelley is my best friend, not my girlfriend, and she's gone for the summer."

"Do you write her lovvveee letters?" Spencer asked.

"Cut it out," Adrian said. "I'll come to your launch party, Willis. I'd hire you to coach me if I had any money."

"You know where to find me!" My scarf blew into my face, but I pushed it back. "I'll leave you with this quote from Walt Disney: 'The way to get started is to quit talking and begin doing.'"

Wow! That quote just popped into my brain. I should write that down and hang it in my office. Looks like I needed a *big* office wall.

Ella crumpled up the invite and tossed it on the ground.

PRO TIP #5:
Stepping in dog poop is dumb.
Littering is dumber.

I picked it up and stuffed the paper into my pocket. I could feel tears coming, but that was okay.

Clarabelle Coburn said that crying helps when you're feeling a feeling. And I bet Michael Morales had some tough steps on his ladder to success. He didn't quit, and neither would I.

"Hey, the Walrus is crying." Ella laughed.

Willis sounded like *walrus*, a fat animal, so that's where the nickname came from. Except you know who else liked walruses? John Lennon, a singer in the Beatles, my very favorite band. Which makes Walrus an *awesome* nickname. Take that, Rudes.

"Hey, what's that smell?" Spencer asked. "Smells like dog poop."

"You probably stepped in something. I gotta go. See ya at the party, Willis." Adrian pedaled away.

Maybe Adrian would be my client someday. Maybe he would even be a friend. But for now, I had to get home to the dozens of kids who were probably knocking on my door.

The bad news: There were not a dozen kids knocking on my door.

The good news: There was one. Ruby Winterton waited on the front porch, holding a hamster cage.

Another possible client!

Logan popped her head out the front door. "Oh, there you are. I heard Ruby talking to Brody at the playground, and I told her to come over. She's your three o'clock appointment. Also, I want 30 percent."

"Not in front of the client," I said through clenched teeth. Inside, my stomach was flipping and flopping. I couldn't believe this moment I'd waited for my whole life, or at least the last two days, was really here. Part of me worried that Ruby wouldn't listen to me. What if I couldn't help her? What if this wasn't my destiny, what if *life* wasn't about destiny at all but just a bunch of random things that randomly happen at random?

But most of me knew this was negative self-talk. I took a deep breath, which was not the best idea, thanks to the poop-shoe situation.

"Hi, Ruby." I shook her hand and looked her right in the eye, like a professional. "I'm Willis Wilbur, Neighborhood Life Coach. What kind of life do you envision for yourself?"

CHAPTER 10

The Guinea Pig!

Ruby shrugged. "What kind of life? Um, I don't know. A regular life?"

"Logan, can you run and get the survey on my desk?"

"I'm not a secretary," Logan said.

"Please?

"Forty percent." She ran inside.

"Let's go into the backyard," I said. "My office is . . . being redesigned." Or it didn't exist. Not yet.

Ruby carried that big old hamster cage with her to the area I had decorated for Mom. I made sure to stay very far away from that evil coffee table. "The survey will help me get to know you. Take it home and fill it out. But for now, let's discuss why you are here."

Ruby unlatched the cage door. A chubby hamster blinked up at me.

"Meet Dog," she said.

"Dog? But he's a hamster."

"*She* is a *guinea pig*." Ruby held out her pet. "I asked my dad for a puppy and I got a guinea pig. Naming her Dog is the closest I'll get to a dog."

"But she's a guinea pig," I said.

"Exactly." Ruby gave her pet a small shake. "And she needs your help."

"The *guinea pig* needs a life coach?"

"Yes. Dog is your client. As you can probably tell, she is sad. Melancholy, my grandma calls it. She's had tons of melancholy lately."

I stared at the animal. I couldn't tell she was sad. Until a minute ago, I couldn't even tell Dog's species.

"You can do it, can't you?" Ruby asked. "Help Dog?"

Probably? I'd talked to animals before, like that cat in the park last Wednesday. The animals didn't talk *back*, but whatever. "Well, Clarabelle Coburn, Life Coach to the Stars, *did* say I should find a guinea pig to practice my coaching, so maybe—"

"Here you go."

I crunched the numbers. Not in the way my mom crunches numbers; this was more about arranging them.

And there was only one number. So far I had one client, and I hadn't even officially signed Margo yet, so really, I had zero. Zero clients meant zero people telling all their friends what an awesome life coach I was. That was zero people thinking, *Hmmm, Willis Wilbur sounds like just the thing I need to change my life. I'll go to him, too.* Which meant I had zero chance of winning that scholarship and finding freedom this summer.

If you multiply a number by zero, you get another zero. Zero was not my favorite number.

"Because I am new, I can coach Dog for free for three sessions," I said. "Then you need to start paying me."

Ruby stuck Dog back into her cage. "Dog is already four years old, and guinea pigs only live to five or six. Seven at best. I'll go with the free package. She might have only three sessions left in her."

Not only did I have to worry about an unhappy

customer, now I had to worry about a dead one.

But I also didn't believe in the word *no*. Well, other times it's a great word—especially after three pieces of pie. But I wasn't going to say no to my destiny, even if it was a different destiny than expected. Maybe I could work with kids *and* their pets. Maybe I'd be the leading neighborhood expert on pet emotional development. I could coach Michael Morales's cat. Maybe my reality show would be *The Pet Coacher!*, and I could do pet coaching spa retreats. Everything could start with one sad Dog. Er, guinea pig.

"I'll do a session with her and see if we're a good fit."

"Great. I have to go to soccer practice." Ruby pulled up her tall socks. "I'll just pick her up after."

"Now?" I panicked. "I can't do it *now*. You still need to fill out the survey. I have to do a personality profile on Dog. I need to buy a scented candle!"

Ruby shrugged. "Just leave her in her cage and grab

her when you're ready. I can pick her up tonight. Or tomorrow, even."

"But my sessions are only fifty minutes."

"Do you have another client to get to?" Ruby asked.

It was clear Logan had already told her the answer. This would be my first appointment.

My shoulders slumped. "Pick her up after soccer."

Ruby slung her soccer bag over her shoulder. She'd brought her bag. Leaving Dog was always the plan.

Was I a life coach or a pet sitter?

"Okay, get happy, Dog!" Ruby said. "I'll see you tonight."

CHAPTER 11

Dog's First Session!

I carried the cage up to my room, a little unsure how Mom would feel about having an animal in the house, even if the animal was there for only the evening. She was allergic to all furry creatures. I slid Dog onto the bed. And then she squeaked.

I had no idea guinea pigs squeaked, or why they squeaked.

So I did the most important thing first: emailed Shelley.

To: shelleygirl928@zmail.com
From: williswilburprofessional@zmail.com
Subject: SQUEAKING GUINEA PIG!

Shells!

I got my first client. My first two clients. One is Margo, which I don't have time to get into. Right now, I need to know everything you know about guinea pigs. Like why do they squeak? And what is the best way to life coach them?
Hurry!

Willis

I kept refreshing my email, but Shelley didn't email me right back. I checked on Dog—she squeaked again! Then I got back on the family computer to look up guinea pigs on a science website that my parents approved. Here are four facts I learned:

1. Guinea pigs are not related to pigs.

2. They do not come from Guinea.

3. Guinea pigs love to spend their time grooming one another and themselves, making them very clean animals to keep as pets.

4. They make lots of different noises when they want to express themselves. They purr when happy, rumble to show dominance, and give a high-pitched squeak when irritated or anxious.

Oh wow. So, the squeaking wasn't good. That's where I needed to start. Except I didn't know the cure for guinea pig anxiety. Mom had anxiety. She went to a doctor and took medicine. She also did yoga.

Wait. Yoga! Perfect!

I laid out my yoga mat next to a hand towel for Dog. I was really proud of myself for coming up with the idea alone, without the help of Shelley or science. Then I turned on soft music and dimmed the lights. Suddenly, my bedroom was a very calm space. Maybe I could do yoga retreats on the side.

Dog stopped squeaking once I took her out of the cage and laid her on her hand towel/yoga mat.

She blinked up at me.

And then she started running.

"Dog!" I jumped to catch her, but Dog disappeared under the dresser.

"Dog?"

I tried everything—nudging Dog out with my plastic sword from Disneyland, patting the floor, playing the Beatles' *The White Album*. I even lined up a trail of nine jelly beans (the greens and purples because I'd already eaten the good ones), but apparently guinea pigs aren't fans of jelly beans. Nothing worked.

I ran downstairs. "Logan! I need the phone. It's an emergency."

"I'm waiting for a phone call," Logan said.

"From who?"

"Anyone. I'm just waiting for it to ring."

I grabbed the flip phone and ran upstairs. Dog was still in distress under the dresser.

I called Shelley. She picked up right away. "Hey, I'm about to surf. What's happening?"

"I'm trying to life coach a guinea pig named Dog, but nothing is working!"

"Willis? You there? Did you say something about a pig dog?"

"Yes! I emailed you!"

"Willis, I can't hear you."

"Ugh, never mind! I'll call you later!"

I flung myself onto the floor. There were so many details Shelley didn't know! It would take the whole session just to fill her in on everything. I'd never done this many things on my own. She picked the wrong time to leave me alone with my destiny.

"Okay, Dog. I'm going to be honest with you. Because honest people live happier, healthier lives. I may not be the best coach for you. I'm not sure how to help you with your melon . . . melon. . . . your sadness. If you can open up to me, I would like to help you set some goals. I know there is an exciting life ahead for you!"

Dog peeked her head out. I almost grabbed her, but she needed to make this move on her own.

"Look, you've already moved so far on this journey! You're halfway to the mat. If you get on your yoga mat, we can work on . . . centering your calm. That sounds smart! Yes, we will center your calm."

Dog waddled over to her mat. She'd accomplished a goal! I gave myself a humongous hug. I'd coached her out from under the dresser. Someday I would share this life coach success story on millions of podcasts and TV interviews. I would write a book called *How to Get Out from Under Life's Dresser*.

"Okay, Dog! Let's work on that calm." I folded my legs into a yoga pose I'd seen my mom do. "We will meditate first. Close your eyes. That helps."

Dog did not close her eyes. But she also didn't run away. She curled up on her mat and stared at me in a way I was learning was very guinea-pig-like.

"Your meditation style is different. That's okay!" I held out my arms, nearly banging my hurt wrist on the dresser. "We are going to visualize our best lives."

Dog didn't like that idea. She sprinted back under the dresser. She stayed there for forty minutes. Maybe I wouldn't write that dresser book after all.

I finally got her into her cage by sticking a spoonful of peanut butter in there.

Ruby showed up an hour later.

"How'd it go?" she asked.

"Dog is a deep thinker," I said.

"Sure." Ruby hoisted the cage onto her hip. "When do you want to meet with her again?"

"I'll look at my schedule."

"He's open tomorrow!" Logan poked her head into the room. "And the next day. And probably the next."

"My sister is so . . . eager." For someone who said she wasn't my secretary, Logan was really getting into my business. "I'm very busy with my launch party. Would Monday morning work?"

"Yeah. I'll come over at eleven." Ruby pulled a Fruit Roll-Up from her pocket. "I got you an extra one at practice. I know this coaching thing is free, but I thought you'd like a tip."

My first payment! Or tip! I'd frame this Fruit Roll-Up (after giving Logan her percent) and hang it in my future office. Future clients would say, *Wow, here I am paying you millions of dollars and you used to get paid in Fruit Roll-Ups?* Then we would laugh because that's what rich people do—laugh about money.

But for now, I needed to figure out how to *make* money. The scholarship committee probably cared about the money part of business, right?

I looked down at my Fruit Roll-Up. That seat at the table was practically mine!

CHAPTER 12

The Office!

"What are you doing?" Dad asked me the next morning at breakfast.

"Sketching my office design."

"Your office?" Dad asked, confused. "Where is your office going?"

"The garage."

Dad dropped the spatula. "The garage? *My* garage? When did that happen?"

I loaded so much sweetness into my smile, I probably got five cavities just from giving it. "We talked about it

97

last night. When you were watching your hockey game. I brought you salsa. Remember?"

"And I told you I'd give up my garage?" Dad asked.

"I asked if I could rent the space. You nodded yes."

"I was nodding at the game!"

The garage was Dad's favorite room in the house. He hung a bunch of band posters on the wall and did stuff with wood in there. It got cold in the winter, but Dad said it put hair on his chest.

"Here's the contract we agreed to."

PRO TIP #6:
Get it in writing.

Dad squinted at the paper. "When did I sign this?"

"Last night. After I brought you the bean dip."

Dad grumbled. "You've got some gumption, kid."

"I've heard that before." I added three more levels

of sugar to my smile. Any more sweetness, and I'd be a lollipop. "Thanks."

"There really isn't another space you could use?"

I didn't answer. I didn't need to.

"Fine. I guess we already made a deal." Dad scanned the contract. "We're doing a three-month lease? And then we'll see how your business looks in the fall?"

"Yes. I might need to find a larger space by then. Once I win the scholarship, I'll have more money to invest in my business. Do you want me to help you clean the garage?"

Dad blinked. "The garage *is* clean."

"Well, the posters need to come down. Everything does. I'm reinventing the space." I was asking for a lot, but dreams don't just fall into your lap! You need to make them happen. And having a nice space to make those dreams happen in sure helped.

Dad slid a hand down his face. "I'll clear it out. The posters need special care."

I jumped up and seized my dad in a hug. Dad smelled like guitar strings and yeasty bread and hesitation. But he loved me, even when I annoyed him.

"I'm headed to the store!" I said. "I'll have to use some of my savings, but this will be worth it. That space will really warm up with a fun rug."

"Sounds good." Dad went back to flipping bacon. I hung my design on the fridge and set off.

Howard's Hardware and General Store was more than a hundred years old and smelled like sawdust and the peppermint candies they sold at the counter. Every few years, someone would try to get a big store like Costco or Target in town, but it never passed. Which was too bad. Small towns are great, but so are the scented candles at Target.

I marched straight to the counter. "I need your help."

"Does your dad need some wood varnish?" a man in faded overalls asked.

"I don't know if he does. I'm building something myself."

"Yeah?" Faded Overalls raised an eyebrow. "You never seemed like the sort. Whatcha building?"

"Dreams! Goals!" I handed Faded Overalls an invite. "Mind if I hang one of these up in the store? Then I have to decide on paint colors. What do you think? Sea-Foam Green or Air Force Blue?"

Faded Overalls pushed the candy jar across the counter. "Have a peppermint, kid."

I stuck the invite on the corkboard and settled into the paint aisle. The quiet time helped me think about my color palette. It is a scientific fact that greens and blues make people feel calm. But maybe I should do yellow, which makes people feel peppy and ready to start a new day. So many thoughts to think!

The store bell jangled. I heard two voices, one a deep old man and one a lady. I couldn't tell her age, but she sneezed a lot.

"What's with the sparkles?" The lady sneezed.

"What's a lie coach?" the man asked.

They were looking at my invite! How perfect. Now I could observe how people might react to my business without them knowing I was there. It was like getting a focus group together for market research in one of those rooms that had a mirror on one side but glass on the other. You know, the rooms that cops and spies used.

"Not an l-i-e coach," The lady said. "A *life* coach. They're someone who helps you through something in life." She sneezed again. Maybe because of the sawdust.

"Who made this kid the expert?"

I mean, I *had* taken the free part of Clarabelle Coburn's course, but these people probably wouldn't understand that.

"I guess *he* did," the lady said. Then they laughed, and the store bell jangled again.

I sat there, in the paint aisle, staring at the rainbow of colors and trying really hard to ignore the negative thought pattern circling in my brain. *What if people don't like sparkles as much as me? What if I'm too inexperienced to talk to other people about their lives? What if I don't get more clients?*

What if I'm not good enough?

Do you believe in signs? I think I might. Because right then, my phone rang. I was sitting there, sorta overwhelmed and unsure. Then my best friend called me!

"Willis!" Shelley said. "Sorry I couldn't talk when you called about pigs. What's going on?"

I didn't want everyone to hear everything that was going on, so I focused on the problem right in front of me. "I'm designing my office. I need to pick a paint color."

"You got an office?" Shelley asked. "You sure discovered your destiny fast! Okay, what colors are we thinking?"

So, Shelley and I talked about the pros and cons of different palettes, until finally we settled on Sea-Foam Green. I could hear her accent more now and her words rolled together. I promised I would call her later to discuss some of the bigger problems I couldn't talk about in public. Then I bought the paint and a candle that didn't smell as good as a Target candle. At least I had an office to paint and an important business to run, and someday those people I overheard would be in a supermarket checkout aisle, looking at a celebrity magazine, and they'd say, *What's a life coach to the stars?* and they'd be talking about me and my large office with a million scented Target candles.

But right then, I had to get home and create a pie chart for Margo's professional playdate.

CHAPTER 13

Margo's Professional Playdate!

To: <u>williswilburprofessional@zmail.com</u>
From: <u>shelleygirl928@zmail.com</u>
Subject: Good luck!

Hi Willis,

It was great talking to you last night. I'm stoked to see how your office turns out. I can't wait to meet Dog.

You'll do a good job with Margo today. Don't be stressed. Maybe you should bring up the First-Grade Episode? Get it out of your system? It's been a long time.

We had an ohana picnic last night. Everyone laughed and had fun. The sky was orange. I love all the tastes and sounds. But I also felt like I don't fit here, not like before. Maybe it's different because we moved to the mainland, ya?

I brought a book and sat outside. Also, I forgot my fidget spinner. The whole time I kept thinking that you would have reminded me to bring it. Then I missed you . . . like really missed you. And I miss us.

Anyway, we went to the batting cages. And we're hiking a waterfall today. So never mind what I said.

Aloha,
Shelley

I wore black shorts and a light blue polo shirt for my appointment.

PRO TIP #7:
Dress for the part.

Today I played the part of a kid who was trying to guide another kid into proper kid activities.

And . . . it was not going great.

First off, Margo had on a business suit.

Second off . . . actually, let's just start with the business suit.

Margo sat with her legs crossed at the picnic bench.

When I got really close, I did a somersault. I would have done a cartwheel, just to show her how a kid having tons of fun looks, but my wrist wouldn't have liked that. In fact, my wrist didn't like the somersault much, either. I had to hold it out weird while I tried to roll forward.

Anyway, Margo laughed. Which was sorta okay. Laughing is part of play, and that's what I was coaching her to do. Well, that's what I thought I was coaching her on, but Margo brought printouts of a spreadsheet.

If you are like me and you don't know what a spreadsheet is, it is a document where data is arranged in rows and columns. At least that's what the internet told me.

"I watched some sample life coaching classes online," Margo said. "You're supposed to ask me what my goals are. Then we'll break down how to accomplish those goals."

"Margo, I know," I said.

"I created a spreadsheet of the playground. We can make sure we play in each sector. Once we've accomplished this first category of achievement, I'd like to move on to viable career paths. Engineering is really my dream, but I can also see myself in Western medicine, maybe pursuing some sort of surgery."

"Let me see that," I said.

For a minute I stood there, staring at the spreadsheet. I had to hand it to Margo, the whole thing was awesomely color coded. Then again, this was also the first spreadsheet I'd ever held because *I was nine.* I had no idea how to make one of these or what to do with it. Which is great, because my niche is thinking like a kid.

Margo clearly had a very long journey of self-discovery ahead of her.

"Right," I said. "Now, as your life coach, let's go over your successes this last week."

"Fun!" Margo ticked things off on her fingers. "Well, I researched age-appropriate play activities. I clicked on a psychology article, then I clicked on another, and then I learned a lot about psychopaths. By the way, neither of us are psychopaths. That's a relief. What else . . ."

"I'm going to stop you right there." I stood up from

the picnic table and stretched a bit. That somersault wasn't good for my neck. "Great successes. Okay, next let's discuss some of the challenges."

"None!" Margo said. "I'm doing fabulously."

"Um, Margo. You made a spreadsheet. On how to *play*."

"Aren't you glad I came prepared?"

"Do you think play is something you can spreadsheet?" I asked.

"Yeah. Because I did."

I tried another approach. "How does living your very adult and businesslike life serve you?"

"I don't understand."

"Okay, let's do an activity," I said. "It's called 'chase.'"

Margo clicked her pen. "Can I write out the rules?"

"No. But if you ever want to see this spreadsheet again, you'll have to catch me." With that, I took off running. I was not very fast, but I zipped around the swings and out of the sandbox. I glanced back to see how far Margo was behind me but . . . she was still sitting at the picnic table.

"You're supposed to catch me!" I called.

"Then what?"

"That's the game." I stopped, trying to catch my breath.

"I'm not paying you to play games," she said.

She's paying me? That's right! Logan already took care of Margo's contract. I was so consumed with the artistic coaching part of this job that I forgot to be businesslike. I walked back over to the table.

When I got close, Margo reached over and grabbed the spreadsheet from me. "Tag!" she said. "Or you're it. Or I got you. I win."

"Margo, that's . . . that's not fair." I really needed to re-read our contract. At least I knew I'd make more than a Fruit Roll-Up. We're talking real money.

"You know, there is a quote from the book *The Little Prince*," I said.

112

Yes, indeed. I'd written a quote in marker on my good arm. Because Willis Wilbur comes prepared.

PRO TIP #8:
When in doubt, quote it out.

"'I have lived a great deal among grown-ups. I have seen them intimately, close at hand. And that hasn't much improved my opinion of them.' Let's close our eyes and really think about that."

Margo nodded. But she didn't close her eyes, and I could tell she wasn't truly absorbing my wisdom about being a kid when you're actually a kid (except for me starting a business—that was a grown-up thing that was totally okay).

Instead, she jumped up. "Read the spreadsheet. It has my obstacle course. I'm definitely going to win. Ready, set, go!" And then she ran over to the slide, taking an unfair head start.

I tried to keep up, but Margo had mapped out this whole thing. And I discovered she was very good at competing, even while exercising in a business suit. She was already at the monkey bars by the time I got through the slide section. Do you know how hard monkey bars are with a wrist brace? I trailed behind her, and it did *not* feel like we were playing.

HOW DO YOU NOT KNOW HOW TO PLAY?

Finally, we flopped onto the grass.

"Okay, now you're supposed to ask me what goals I'd like to set for next week." Margo pulled her planner out of her backpack and started writing down more and more plans.

I sat up. My sides hurt. Right then, I wished Shelley never went to Hawaii and we were at band camp. Shelley said they served really good spaghetti in the camp cafeteria. That had to be more fun than trying to figure out how to life coach someone who seemed to be life coaching me.

And also . . . I was a little annoyed that Margo still hadn't said anything about why we weren't friends. About that first-grade thing.

All of this led to something that got in the way of my date with destiny: *doubt*. Did Clarabelle Coburn ever experience it? Were any of the other BOO kids in Green Slope struggling, too? Seriously, mastering the sousaphone seemed a lot easier than this.

I breathed some more. Lots more. Told myself a few more motivational quotes. Grounded myself in the moment.

"Here's your homework," I said. "No more spreadsheets. No more planning. You need to find an activity you enjoy and just let yourself get lost in it."

"But I *enjoy* spreadsheets."

"Look, I'm the life coach here. And I'm telling you—your homework is to try something new without making a spreadsheet. Now . . . hand me your planner."

Margo listened, but she seemed bothered.

I still didn't know if I was doing this job right. I never had problems like this with Shelley. We met up at each other's houses and just . . . played. We didn't really think about it. All Margo seemed to do was *think about it*. I wondered if she ever stopped thinking and just felt feelings.

Honestly. I wouldn't say this in a magazine interview or anything, but I was starting to wonder if this was an impossible professional relationship.

CHAPTER 14

Dog's Second Session!

To: shelleygirl928@zmail.com
From: williswilburprofessional@zmail.com
Subject: Re: Good luck!

Shelley,

My appointment with Margo went all right, but we can talk about it later. Same with my next appointment with Dog (even though I still have to plan out my professional outfit).

Are you okay? It seems like maybe you're having a hard time? I miss you SO MUCH. But I also want you to be happy while you are in Hawaii. I'm here if you want to talk. I'm going to keep calling you, even if the cell coverage is bad or Logan won't give me the phone or you are surfing or I am life coaching. It's okay if you don't answer.

Maybe this is too life coach-y of me, but oh well. I just want you to know you are a very wonderful person. Like if there was a Wonderful Person Contest, you would win. The prize would be an expensive sports car or probably something smaller, like a blue ribbon. You would also win a Creative Person Award. Remember all the games you invented for us—taco tag, art soccer, and reading chase (which I think was really a sneaky way for you to get me to read more)?

Maybe . . . maybe you have a date with destiny, too. Maybe your destiny right now is different from mine, and maybe it's figuring out how to use all your wonderfulness and creativity when you're in a new situation? Or maybe it's something else. You tell me.

Aloha,
Willis

Ruby showed up fifteen minutes late for Dog's second session.

"Hey." She practically dropped Dog's cage on the front porch. "I've got to go. Dog's been running around and squeaking a lot."

"That's because she's anxious," I said.

"Huh?" Ruby bit at a hangnail. "I told you. She's sad. Get that fixed, okay? I'll be back tonight."

"Tonight?" I stepped onto the porch. "Ruby, this isn't

119

how life coaching works. Especially *free* life coaching."

Ruby clapped her hands together. "I'm going over to my cousin's house, and I can't take Dog. And I don't want to leave her alone since she's acting weird. Please?"

Dog skittered back and forth across the cage. My client clearly needed help.

Dog and I went up to my room so Mom wouldn't know there was a rodent around. After I turned down the lights to a soothing level and made my face look very soothing, too, I got close-up to her cage.

"Hello, Dog. I'm excited to work with you today. Normally, I would ask you where you are right now and where you want to go. You know, mentally or emotionally. But you can't answer that because you are a guinea pig. We're going to have to get creative."

Next came the part I was sorta nervous about because of the whole Dresser Disaster last time.

"Now, I am going to open your cage. I want you to think of this cage as someplace safe. It is not a place you need to escape. This is your home. When I open the cage, you get to stay in the safe space. Then we will do some games that help you grow. And you can earn treats!"

It was too bad I wasn't filming this so I could make an instructional video. Actually, I could make a whole series and sell them online. I needed a backup plan in case I didn't win the scholarship. I'd have to explore other ways to become a legend/get out of day camp. The pet coach idea was still possible. Kind of.

Next came music. We started with a Beatles song called "Piggies," which is a cute nickname for guinea pigs. This song was about Dog! Extra perfect and happy.

"Have you seen the little piggies . . ."

I opened the cage.

Dog sprinted right out.

121

"Dog!" I caught her this time.

Dog shook in my hands.

I looked into her eyes. She looked into mine. That's when we saw each other's souls.

There are hard truths businesspeople need to face when they are growing their businesses. This was a huge, sharp, melancholy one.

I couldn't help Dog. Not as a life coach and not how she needed to be helped. We could do session after session, and she'd probably still run under my dresser.

And I'm not sure Ruby would even care or notice. She just wanted me to "fix" her pet. But you can't ask a guinea pig to suddenly not be a guinea pig.

"Come on. Let's go downstairs."

I put Dog inside a large cardboard box with some blankets. Logan came home and colored the box with markers. Dog relaxed. She did a few tricks, like standing for a treat and running through a little hoop. Logan didn't fight with me or ask for a higher percent. We just played. Too bad Margo wasn't there—I could have worked with two clients at once.

Mom came in from the garage. "Hey, Willis? Can you come here for a second?"

"I can't!" I called. "I'm life coaching!"

"You're life coaching a hamster?"

"A guinea pig. But I guess I'm not really coaching her anymore."

"Why don't you have Logan watch the animal for

123

a bit? I'll help you paint the garage." Mom sneezed. "And then you'll have to take the hamster upstairs. I can't handle furry creatures."

Logan gathered Dog into her arms and rocked her like a baby. "I've always wanted a pet! We're going to be best friends."

I stepped into the garage and into another world.

"What is . . . what is this?"

Mom and Dad stood in the middle of the design I'd sketched out yesterday and stuck on the fridge. The Sea-Foam Green paint job was complete. There were two white chairs with bright pillows. There was the fluffy rug, the glowing lamp, the coffee table covered in magazines, the fern, the large mirror, and bookcases, empty and waiting for a future library of life coaching books. All I had to do was move the white sheet on the wall and maybe hang a Michael Morales real estate calendar in the corner.

You know, I bet Michael Morales's office didn't look *half* this fancy.

"You . . . you did this for me?" I asked.

Dad shrugged. "Your wrist is sprained. No way you could have put those bookcases together."

"We used the money you made designing the patio," Mom said. "The rest of the cost we consider an investment."

My words stuck in my throat. "Thank you."

My parents shone like one of my humongous lightbulb moments. Dad gave me this back-slap-hug thing. Maybe that's hopeful, calling it a hug. He's not an A+ snuggler like Mom, who is basically a love octopus.

"Last thing." Mom yanked the white sheet away, revealing her Big Surprise. "Ta-da!"

Behind the sheet was a large piece of wood with the words "Willis Wilbur: Neighborhood Life Coach" written in fancy letters.

"I had an extra piece of birchwood." Dad shrugged again. "Still needs varnish."

Sometimes it felt like *I* was Mom and Dad's guinea pig because I was the first kid and Dad always said, *We're still learning.* Mom said, *Parenting doesn't come with a manual,* which is kind of silly because who needs manuals with the internet around.

But tonight it didn't feel like my parents were trying to teach me or even change me. I felt like enough. I flipped to a fresh page on my yellow legal pad and added:

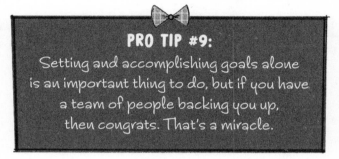

PRO TIP #9:
Setting and accomplishing goals alone
is an important thing to do, but if you have
a team of people backing you up,
then congrats. That's a miracle.

"Now get in there and start vacuuming," Mom said. "I'm going to sneeze my face off. Let's have your next client be a human, deal?"

I hugged my mom. "Deal."

CHAPTER 15

The Launch Party!

7 THINGS EVERY LAUNCH PARTY NEEDS TO BE A HUGE SUCCESS!

(Also from *Working Parents Weekly* magazine.
I bought a subscription.)

1. Make Invitations

Way ahead of you. Done!

2. Pick the Right Venue

My awesome new office. Double done!

3. Hire Staff

Dad helped with the food. Mom hosed down the driveway and blew up balloons. Logan promised to gather phone numbers and to sign up clients and not ask for more money.

4. Invite Future Clients

I'd done this all over town.

5. Invest in Your Party, Invest in Your Business

I spent thirty-two dollars and eight cents on food and decorations. Someday I would buy Important Life Coaching Books, but for now, I filled the bookcase with Mom's romance novels, making a very colorful display.

6. Buy Some Swag

Swag is cool stuff you give away for free to remind

people of your brand. Mom splurged on red "Willis Wilbur: Neighborhood Life Coach" stress balls. Every kid in the neighborhood would squeeze my name and remember me!

7. Be a Great Host

This one turned out to be hard. And not hard in the way I thought it would be hard. Let me tell you why . . .

Like most parties, the first thirty minutes of my launch was Awkward with a million capital *As*. Things started off with my family sitting in the garage/office, listening to Beatles records and eating hummus. Then Ruby called and said she couldn't make it. Margo was one of the first to arrive. She sat next to me on the couch, chattering.

"The green paint is really soothing. You have such fantastic style! This rug is festive. You should start a design business on the side. Oh, I like your suspenders. Are those loafers new?"

I had on a floral bow tie, blue suspenders, and my cousin's hand-me-down shoes. My hair took me twenty minutes to get just right. Then I put on aftershave, even though I didn't actually shave. It was probably the nicest I'd ever looked ever. Hopefully, Margo wasn't the only one to notice.

"Interior design is such a smart idea. I'm good at smart ideas," Margo said. "I could be your business partner. I mean, maybe. I'm in a lot of clubs right now. And college prep classes. I also had some ideas for our next playdate. Have you heard of academic paintball?"

My stress ball was a really nice thing to have handy.

"Margo! We're glad that you're here." Logan sat next to Margo and smiled. "Let's discuss your next session. Willis, why don't you go mingle?"

My sister was getting a raise. You know, just as soon as I made money.

I tried extra hard to be a Smart and Professional Life

Coach, but this business stuff was tough! The party was boringer than the boringest boring that ever boringed. But then two good things happened:

1. A cookie bouquet arrived! It was from the Kalanis. The note said, "Willis! We are so proud of you for finding your destiny. Aloha!"

Wow! The best present from my other half. I almost cried, which is fine because there is nothing wrong with crying, except I looked snazzy and I didn't want my face to get splotchy. And I was really glad I didn't have a splotchy face when the next thing happened.

2. Adrian James finally showed up.

My heart skipped a beat. If Adrian was here, the rest of the neighborhood would follow. One business article said to invite "the right people." Adrian was so right, there was no way the party could go wrong.

"Willis! My man." Adrian gave me a high five. "Sweet setup."

It *was* a sweet setup. I couldn't believe we'd pulled it off in a week. My family came through for me. When I write a life coaching book someday, I will dedicate it to them. Or at least give them a free copy. "Well, as the Beatles would say, I had 'a little help from my friends.'"

"What's that?" Adrian asked.

"It's a Beatles song."

"Is that this music that's playing?" Adrian asked.

Okay, so not every nine-year-old or even ten-year-old listened to the Beatles. They were an old band, but they were a *classic* band. And the song playing was a popular one. Anyway, Adrian James showed up! This was huge.

"Do you want some pigs in a blanket?" I asked.

"Dude, look at this food!" Adrian whipped out a phone. "I've got to tell my friends. Hey, 'Tell My Friends.' Is that a Beatles song, too?"

"Um, no."

Within a few minutes there were more kids. Then more. Soon, the party flowed out of the garage and onto the driveway.

I ran from group to group, handing out stress balls and business cards. This was the party I dreamed of creating (just look at my party dream board). The room

was packed with future clients. Well, mostly future clients. Some kids were there only for the cheese platter.

One kid looked at the stress ball and then at me. "What's a life coach?"

"It's a person who encourages clients on school or life goals."

"What's a Willis Wilbur?"

"Me?" I said. "That's . . . me."

"Huh." The kid shoved the ball into his pocket and walked away.

That's okay. The kid would pull out that stress ball during a stressful moment. And boom! There I'd be, ready to help. Marketing genius.

Logan ran up to me. "We have an egg situation on the front porch."

"Are we out of deviled eggs?" I asked.

"It's . . . worse than that."

We walked to the front porch. "The egg situation," as Logan called it, was actually an egg *disaster*. Someone had thrown at least a dozen eggs at our house.

I poked at a shattered shell. I suddenly understood Dog's melancholy. "Did you check the doorbell camera?"

My parents installed a doorbell camera last year after the neighborhood experienced some vandalism.

They'd never needed to "catch" someone before.

Until now.

"I looked," Logan said.

"Who did it?" I was pretty sure I knew the answer.

"Um, it was the Rudes."

I closed my eyes.

Enough. I'd had enough, and I was going to do something about it.

CHAPTER 16

Talk to the Rudes!

Ella and Spencer were already at the party, shoving cream puffs into their faces. Which meant they had egged my house, parked their bikes, then walked right into the garage like nothing had happened.

Steam shot out of my ears like in the cartoons. I marched up to Ella and held up an eggshell. "Why do you spread your negative energy around like this?"

Ella swallowed her cream puff. "What?"

"Do you know my job is to help people be their best selves? Even when there is an obstacle? Well, *you're* my obstacle." I threw the eggshell onto the floor, which luckily hit the concrete and not my fun rug. "This is the advice I would give a client who is being bullied. I would encourage them to ignore the bully, which I have done. I would hope my client would avoid the bully, which I have done. I would tell them to communicate in a firm, unemotional way. And to look the bully in the eye. *I am looking you in the eye.*"

"We aren't bullying you." Spencer yawned. "We're just messing around. Besides, we came to your party. See, we're friends."

"How many free Starbursts did you shove in your pocket?" I asked.

Spencer blushed. "You invited us to the party, you know."

It was true. I had. And part of me felt bad for them. They worked really hard to be "cool." We could probably even figure out why they bullied other kids so much.

140

But this wasn't about them right now. This was *my* party. They teased me constantly. They egged my house.

The bullies had to go.

"I did invite you, but now I need you to leave," I said.

"Are you serious, Walrus?" Ella asked.

"It's *Willis*." Margo stepped next to me and folded her arms across her chest. "And yes. I think he is."

Wow, I felt powerful having someone next to me. Especially a powerful person like Margo. It almost erased the First-Grade Episode. Almost.

Spencer shrugged. "Okay, everyone. Let's move the party to my house. We have a pool. And a trampoline."

The bulk of the kids stood there frozen for a minute. But when Ella and Spencer left, a lot of them decided to follow. Most of the food was gone, and I hadn't planned a game. Besides, it's hard to compete with a pool *and* a trampoline.

Adrian slapped me on the back. "I'm leaving. But can I have one of those surveys?"

"What for?" I asked. I was still kind of buzzing from standing up to Spencer and Ella. I'd learned a lot from those Clarabelle Coburn videos. Even if I never coached another person, I'd sure coached myself. I could probably start an anti-bullying program with Michael Morales in the town community center, which would go so well that other cities would start to copy us. Then we'd be guests on famous talk shows together. Then they'd offer us our own show—*Michael M. & Willis W. in the Morning.*

"I'm thinking about signing up. I like how you handled Ella and Spencer." Adrian shuffled his feet. "I bet you could help me with a problem I'm having, too."

Within five more minutes, the garage was close to empty. The party was over.

I didn't care.

I had to scrape off egg yolk from the front porch.

I didn't care.

I had to clean up the party mess, including vacuuming chips off my new rug.

I didn't care.

Logan collected five phone numbers and signed up two clients: Adrian and a very tall third grader.

And I was twenty miles beyond excited. I was a nine-year-old with my very own business! I had real, live

143

human clients! And no one asked me where Shelley was. I missed her, completely, but . . . I was my own person today.

Just Willis.

That night, our family ate celebratory fruit salad. On Friday I would take all this experience into the BOO scholarship presentation. Sure, I hadn't made much money, but I'd gained so much *gumption*.

Once they heard these stories, the committee would clap and cheer and go into the hallway to tell everyone else: *You might as well go home, Willis already clinched it.* I would be in commercials for BOO and talk with other BOO kids and maybe start a BOO camp for kids who wanted to build businesses.

I would never have to go to another boring summer camp again, not when I was so close to legend status. So, so close.

CHAPTER 17

Margo's Second Professional Playdate!

To: williswilburprofessional@zmail.com
From: shelleygirl928@zmail.com
Subject: My destiny

Willy Bear (haha, I miss hearing your mom call you that),

Yesterday we hung out with all my family! I didn't bring my book. I won at UNO and stuffed myself on kalua pig. So ono! Today I'm going to a movie with my cousin and her friends. I've really been thinking about what you said about making a date with destiny.

Honestly, I don't think I need one. A date. I think my destiny will find me when we are both ready. You and I are different that way. It takes me a while to warm up when I'm in a new place or with new people. I have to honor that. Plus, I'm not always going to have you around to remind me to wear sunscreen or to share an inside joke. I love Shellis/Willey, but also being just Shelley is cool, too.

And aww, mahalo for the 20 postcards with all your favorite inspirational quotes. That's a lot of stamps! My favorite quote was this: "The most beautiful discovery true friends make is that they can grow separately without growing apart." (by Elisabeth Foley, whoever that is).

Loads of ALOHA!
Shelley

At my launch, Henry Po invited me to his Surf's Up Fun Zone birthday party. Henry was lucky that my schedule was open. Someday last-minute invites like this just won't work. Not only would my schedule be booked months in advance, but I'd get invites from people who wanted me to walk them down the aisles at their weddings or take them to a high school dance or go tandem skydiving with them. And although I'd always want to connect with my fans, I couldn't go to a million birthday parties!

Surf's Up Fun Zone was beach-themed, probably so kids could forget they lived in a landlocked state. Really, everyone in Colorado was always Rockies *this*

and mountains *that*. I was extra on board with the under-the-sea bowling alley that served pineapple ice cream.

Margo was also invited to the party, which gave us the perfect opportunity to be around other kids together. We sat in a sticky booth in the pizza restaurant right next to the laser tag. We agreed to meet thirty minutes early so Margo could prepare for the party.

I'd read through Margo's contract and survey, which I wanted to frame but figured I would wait until I was famouser, especially since she probably wanted her details to stay private. Margo agreed to pay me five dollars an hour for my consulting! Today was the first time I'd ever been paid. I didn't even care that she paid me mostly in quarters. In fact, I could use a few of those quarters at the arcade. Look, I wasn't a machine. I couldn't save *every* penny that I made.

"Okay. First things first," I said. "I need you to remember that I'm the coach here."

"Of course." Margo frowned. "Although . . . maybe you should lose the bow tie when the party starts."

"It's part of my brand," I said.

Margo shrugged, like she didn't care. But she really did.

"Why don't you tell me about any successes you've had since our last appointment?" I asked.

"I went to your party and I talked to five new people," Margo said. "About kid things. Or I think we were talking about kid things. Like hopscotch. I think I should master hopscotch."

"That's great to hear," I said. "Where did your love for hopscotch start?"

"I don't know. Shelley and I used to chalk hopscotch on my driveway." She looked down for a second. "I miss that. I miss her."

148

"Me too." I bit into my pizza.

"Do you think that's a normal reason for two people to hang out? Because they are friends with the same person?"

"We're hanging out because I'm a paid, professional, kid life coach, and today we are going to engage in a fun childhood-focused activity."

Margo wiped her face with a napkin. "Yeah, totally."

Then we were quiet for a few minutes. Like too many minutes. Not only was I new to life coaching, but I didn't exactly go to birthday parties every day. It was a good thing Margo was there. I had a hunch she wasn't on a million invite lists, either.

"Want to call Shelley?" I asked.

Margo grinned. "I'm so glad you asked."

Margo had a fancy camera on her phone. When Shelley answered, it was the first I'd seen her in days. My best friend looked very smiley and relaxed. Whew. The breathing exercises I'd sent her must be working.

"Aloha! Hey, you guys are hanging out *together*?"

"Does it look like we're in Hawaii?" Margo asked, holding up the phone to the mural of a wave.

Shelley snorted. "Totally! Are you having fun?"

Margo and I exchanged a look behind the phone. Were we? We weren't exactly here for the fun. Or I guess Margo was paying me to *make* her have fun. Forced fun isn't the highest level of fun. But I hadn't forgotten that she'd stood up for me at my launch party. And that she knew how to make a mean spreadsheet. I was sorta kinda starting to like her. Not in *that* way. But you know.

"Yeah," Margo and I said at the same time, then started laughing.

Shelley grinned. "Cool. You guys should go to the fake sandpit. I'll go to the beach. It'll be like we're all hanging out together!"

"Tubular!" Margo said.

"Hang loose," I said.

150

"Aloha!" Shelley said.

We hung up the phone.

"There is no way in a million years I'm going in that gross sandpit," Margo said.

"Duh. We have life coaching to do. I didn't wear a bow tie for nothing."

I came prepared for this party. Not only had I learned what a spreadsheet was, but I actually made one. Not on my computer, but with markers and stuff. I was extra excited to show Margo. I'd ranked each activity based on Best Stuff for Nine-Year-Olds. Here's the list.

Now . . . guess what Margo picked. Just guess.

Arcade games!		
Bowling!		
Ropes course!		
Bumper boats!		
Laser tag!		
Minigolf (don't love this one, please don't pick)		

151

CHAPTER 18

The First-Grade Episode!

Margo took one look at my spreadsheet and sighed. "I guess . . . minigolf."

"*Minigolf?* You know golf is an adult sport? So you're basically doing the smaller version of an adult sport."

"It's part of my brand."

At least the golf course was beach-themed with sandpits, palm trees, and even cute cartoon crabs. Tiki torches lit the entrance. Margo didn't seem to notice any of those details. She was really focused on getting the golf ball into the hole. She even kept score.

"Willis, you hit the ball already. You can't just hit it again."

"I didn't like the direction it was going." I pointed at Margo. "You know, let's talk about the direction *you* are going! How are you being more of a kid right now? Every other kid at the party picked better kid activities. I mean, air hockey would work better than this."

Margo shot a ball. It went right into the hole. I think that's called "a one in the hole." "Why do you need me to act a certain age so much?"

I swung, but I missed the ball. See? This game is not for kids. So much concentration. "I don't need you to. I thought *you* needed to."

Margo leaned on her golf stick. I think it's called "a club." "But I'm superfine with the way I am. I work hard and play hard. Like . . . I'm awesome."

"True."

154

"Isn't a life coach supposed to help you be your best self? Not change you?"

It had been a while since I'd watched Clarabelle Coburn's instructional video, but this sounded like something she would say. I was so consumed with trying to coach Margo the way I thought she needed, I ignored what she wanted. Which was kind of what I did with Dog, and that hadn't worked, either.

Margo liked planning and learning and dreaming about her future. She liked different things from other kids her age but, hey, so did I. Why should I ever try to fix that? Margo was right. She really was awesome.

PRO TIP #10:
The customer is always right—
most of the time.

I was never going to get my own talk show if I kept this up. I reminded myself to take notes of this conversation before my scholarship meeting tomorrow. I almost felt bad that Margo was paying me for this, but only almost.

"You're right!" I said. "I'm learning just as much from you." And then I can't really say why I did the next thing. Maybe because I was starting to realize Margo wasn't horrible, and I needed to clear the air. "Hey, Margo? You don't have to pay me for this next part. But I wanted to talk to you about . . ." My hands were starting to sweat. I never talked about the First-Grade Episode. I couldn't believe I was bringing it up now. "Do you remember in first grade, when our teacher gave out awards after we'd reached something important?"

"Uh, yeah. I guess."

"Do you remember how you always got fastest math whiz? Like, no matter what, you were always faster than everyone?"

She shrugged. "Yeah."

"Well, one time I was really close, like two points behind you, and Mr. Giovanni wanted to give me the math whiz award, and you said no—you should get it because you were still the fastest. And . . . that really bothered me. I worked really hard for that award. Like all year."

"So did I," she said. "Look, I don't know what to say. Do you want me to apologize?"

I'd waited for this moment for more than two and a half years. Yes! I wanted Margo to see that she took something away from me. I wanted her to give other people a chance to shine. I wanted . . . I wanted . . . to stop holding on to the award I never got. "Nah. I was just thinking about it. Maybe you can write your college essay about it someday."

"Or I'll just write about my weird friend, Willis."

Well, fine. If we're being honest, I sorta liked that

Margo called me that. A weird friend. And I liked letting go of that old hurt and letting in a new person. No more stewing over the First-Grade Episode. Wow, it's like I gave myself a life coaching session while coaching Margo. And I didn't have to pay for it.

I putted another ball. The ball jumped off the grass and into the fake water. Minigolf was maybe one of the funnest games I'd ever played.

But we're not going to tell Margo that, right?

CHAPTER 19

The Scholarship Presentation!

When Logan was five, Mom took her to Disneyland. The night before, Logan jumped on my bed, repeating every exciting activity, every ride and character. She actually threw up; she was so excited. Or maybe it was all that bed jumping.

I never understood that kind of excitement until Friday, when I sat outside the BOO scholarship presentation. I folded and unfolded my notes over and over again until the creases ripped. The teen boy next to me tapped his foot and the almost-a-teen girl hummed. I put on my headset and thought positive affirmations.

My life is full of abundance.

I love and approve of myself.

Doors are opening for me now.

This scholarship is my destiny, and I will become a legend.

"Excuse me." Someone tapped me on the shoulder.

I opened my eyes. It was a businesswoman in a yellow pantsuit. She smelled like fruity perfume and something else. What was it? Oh, yes. Success.

"Are you Willis Wilbur?" Yellow Pantsuit asked.

I was pretty sure she wasn't asking for my autograph. Pretty sure.

"I am indeed."

She smiled. "The scholarship committee is ready for you."

I let out a long breath. I'd been preparing my whole

life for this moment. Well, two weeks. Two very long, very busy weeks.

The scholarship committee sat at a long table, just like I'd imagined. Michael Morales sat in the middle. His hair was very shiny, and his suit very ironed. There were five other members. They had different products on the table. Jam. T-shirts. Some plastic thing shaped like a waffle.

I didn't have a product. I *was* the product.

"Hello. I'm Willis Wilbur. Neighborhood Life Coach." I shook each business owner's hand and gave everyone a stress ball.

"Hello, Willis." A woman in a green scarf smiled. Her front tooth was crooked in a cheerful way. Her name was June La.

PRO TIP #11:
Make sure to remember your interviewer's name.

"You have three minutes to tell us about your business. Then we will ask three questions. Are you ready?"

Of course I was ready. Just look at my bow tie.

I had a PowerPoint that included screenshots of my website, video from the launch party, pictures of Dog and Margo, and even a few personal affirmations. The businesspeople nodded in the right parts and laughed in the right parts. One even wiped a tear away at the end.

"I can tell you've worked hard to build your business," June said. "We have some questions for you. Can you tell us how much revenue you've brought in?"

This was a new word. "Revenue?"

"How much money your business made."

"Oh. Sure. None."

"None?" she asked. "Can you explain?"

I fiddled with my bow tie. It was on pretty tight. "I've invested all of my money into the business.

But I've been open for only two weeks. Well, four days if you count from the launch. The guinea pig client was offered free services so I could practice. Margo's payment went toward business expenses. But good news! I have two new clients booked next week. I project a profit happening soon."

"Makes sense." June scribbled some notes on paper. So did the other business owners.

"Next question." Yellow Pantsuit smiled. She hadn't told me her name. "What is unique about your business?"

"Have you ever met anyone named Willis Wilbur before?" I asked.

The group shook their heads.

"Have you ever met a nine-year-old life coach?"

Again, head shakes.

"Then that answers your question. I found my niche." I waved my injured wrist in the air. "Nobody else is working the kid coaching market."

163

More notes were scribbled. This time with smiles.

Michael Morales leaned back in his seat and stared at me like I was a question and the only answer came from staring. I really wanted to cross the room and give him a fist bump. "I'm Michael Morales."

"I know," I said. "I sit on your benches all the time."

He grinned. "That's great to hear. I'll get you an autograph."

"Wow, really?" My sister would be extra jealous.

"Anything for a fan." Michael winked. "Are your parents looking to sell their house?"

"Michael," June said. "We're not here for *your* business."

Michael shook his head. "Of course. Local celebrity moment. You understand."

None of the other business owners smiled at Michael Morales. Maybe because his smile never turned off? He sipped his coffee.

"Are you going to ask Willis a question?" Yellow

Pantsuit asked, frowning at him.

Michael Morales leaned back in his seat. "Nah. Willis has gumption, dontcha, kid?"

I didn't know what to say. Gumption was on the BOO flyer, so obviously it was important. But it felt like Michael Morales didn't really care what I had to say. Maybe he was just there to smile a lot? Maybe I didn't want to host a talk show with him anymore.

"Final question, Willis," Yellow Pantsuit said. "How does your business contribute to our community?"

I spread my hands wide. "I have *neighborhood* right in the title. And I believe that a good community business focuses on service. At some point I will make money from helping people. But that doesn't change what I am doing—helping. When I first started I tried to force clients to be what I wanted. But I learned to listen and guide. Kids in Green Slope will learn to overcome their fears and accomplish big things. It's my gift to my community, but it's also a gift for me because I've learned to *be* myself when I'm *by* myself. You probably don't understand that part, but that's because you haven't met my best friend, Shelley. Anyway . . . I really like this quote from the boxer Muhammad Ali: 'Service

to others is the rent you pay for your room here on earth.' Thank you."

Boom. If I had a microphone, I would have dropped it right then.

Date. Destiny.

Done.

CHAPTER 20

The Big News!

The business owners clapped as I floated out of the room. Then I floated around the neighborhood for the next hour. I even let Mom talk me into floating at the neighborhood pool. Float, float, float.

The sky was so blue, the trees so green, my heart so full. There wasn't a word to describe this sense of accomplishment. *Happy* wasn't big enough. *Joyful* wasn't round enough.

There was a note from Logan on my bedroom door when I got home.

"Some scholarship guy called. Here's his number."

Today was Logan's day with our cell phone. Since she was nowhere to be found, Mom finally let me use her phone.

I walked over to the magical bench where this had all started. Out of respect, I did not sit on Michael Morales's face. Instead, I sat on his phone number, which was the same phone number I dialed with a shaky hand.

"Hello, this is Willis Wilbur." I blew out a breath. "Just returning your phone call."

"Oh! Hello! This is Michael Morales, of Morales Homes and Enterprises."

"Michael . . . *the* Michael Morales?" I asked.

"Oh, that's right. You're a fan." There was some sort of commotion in the background. "Give me a second. I'm just helping my kids."

I tapped my foot while Michael instructed his kids

to put their bikes away before he took them away. Wow, he sounded just like my dad. It's nice to know a celebrity could be just like regular people.

Finally, he got on the phone. "Okay, Willis. First off, the committee wanted me to tell you we were very impressed with your business savvy."

"Thank you." I reminded myself to look up the word *savvy*.

"And personally, I think the bow tie is a good look on you."

I KNEW IT.

"Unfortunately . . ."

With that one word my stomach dropped. My soul shriveled. My destiny disappeared.

"We decided to go with a candidate who has a more established business. Jam, actually. I love jam. But I want you to know, this is not a failure."

Tell that to the rest of my summer.

I leaned forward, resting my forehead on my wrist brace.

"You've created a business," Michael Morales said. "I didn't start my first business until I was fourteen. And now look at me. This is one rung on your ladder to success."

"Thank you for your time," I said. I was not crying. Not yet. "Best of luck in your future, Mr. Morales."

"And Willis?" Michael Morales added.

I had to get off the phone. Rejection was not something that should last this long.

"I told my son about your business. He's twelve. He would like to book an appointment."

And then the tears slipped out. I had to cover my mouth to keep from letting out a sob. Clarabelle Coburn may have said to feel your feelings, but she didn't understand what it was like to feel so many good and bad feelings at the exact same time.

"Are you still there?" Michael Morales asked.

"Yes." I swallowed. "Sounds good. Have him—" I stopped. Dried my eyes. Swallowed again. "Have him. Call and make. An appointment. Goodbye."

I stretched out on Michael Morales's bench. I would never have my own bench. I was not a legend, and I was never going to be a legend. No one would name a wing in the hospital after me or tell all their friends they know me, even when they didn't. I had Michael Morales *on the phone*, and I didn't do something smart like pitch more business ideas.

I was a regular nine-year-old with a box of leftover stress balls. I might as well eat crayons or watch the wind blow or whatever it is kids without gumption do. Actually, I wouldn't have time. Now that I lost the scholarship, Mom would sign me up for Jell-O wrestling or underwater basket weaving.

I called Shelley. She answered on the first ring.

"How'd it go?" she asked.

I shook my head, but of course she couldn't see me shaking my head. "I didn't. Get it."

"Oh Willis."

And then she just listened as I cried some more on the phone. I'll admit it—I whined a little, and thought about drawing a mustache on Michael Morales (but didn't). She listened. She's good at that. Even though she was an ocean away, she felt really close.

And we talked about her family and adventures and journey. We talked about how we'd both managed to find ourselves while still missing each other. We talked about name ideas for the next time we ate grapes.

I felt a little better as I walked home. I was about to go inside to tell my mom the news, to let her dump a Summer Fun Plan on me, when I noticed a package on the front porch. A loaf of fresh bread with a jar of jam. Faye Limbaco's jam, the scholarship winner. (Yes, the jam was *that* good. The secret is picking the strawberries at just the right time.)

Here's what the note said:

Willis,

I was really mean. I mean, really, REALLY mean. I could tell you all the things that happened to me that made me decide to be mean. But they are just excuses, and none of them are your fault. I shouldn't have egged your house or made fun of your body. My mom said I'm better than that and I am. I made bad choices, and I will do better in the future. I'm very sorry.

~Ella

PS The eggs actually happened because Spencer and I were in a fight with each other. It started with a trip to the grocery store, and then we forgot the cinnamon and started doing dares and Spencer has bad aim. Long story, no excuse.

PPS Spencer and I actually like each other. Like, *like* like each other. I don't know if you knew that.

PPPS At least I think we still like each other.

PPPPS Do you do any couples coaching? Our problems obviously aren't about you. We need to work on ourselves.

PPPPPS Maybe I'll just call and book an appointment.

I dropped the note. Not because I was mad or happy. It was great that Ella apologized, but she still had to prove she'd changed. And I did *not* want to think about Ella and Spencer liking each other, or how egging had anything to do with a crush. I dropped the note because I had to get somewhere, and *fast*.

I ran back into the house and handed my mom her phone.

"I didn't win the scholarship," I said. "And now I have to go."

"I'm sorry, Bug." Mom hugged me. I let her. It's easier if you don't resist her octopus hugs. "We need to talk."

Ugh, there was no escaping the camps/sports/sports camps. Within a few moments my fate would be sealed. My soul would be bound. "I know. There's just something important I have to do first."

"But, Will . . ."

"I'll be right back!"

I zipped right out the door. I could accept whatever fate was laid before me if I just saw something through first. Otherwise, I would never know if life coaching was my life's calling or simply something to delay the Summer Fun Torture.

You see, that thing Ella said about couples coaching gave me a perfect idea. I just hoped my client was home.

CHAPTER 21

My Professional Breakthrough!

I ran around the pond. I ran through the soccer field. I ran over the mountain biking jumps and under the bridge and over to Ruby's house. I stopped to catch my breath (because remember, my breath is not as fast as my legs). Then I knocked on Ruby's door with my good hand.

Ruby cracked open the door. "What do you want?"

"Can I please do one more session with Dog?"

"I'll bring her tomorrow."

"I might not *have* tomorrow. Can we meet now?"

"Fine. But I'm not paying." Ruby opened the door.

"She's upstairs. I'm playing a video game."

"I need you to come with me."

Ruby moaned. "But I just made it to the next level."

"You paused it, right? This will only take a minute."

Ruby's room was . . . surprising. Every inch of wall was covered in dog posters. Even her bedding had a puppy print. Dog (the guinea pig) was shoved into a corner of the room. I walked right over to her cage.

"Have a seat in the middle of the room, Ruby."

Ruby flopped down. I set Dog in Ruby's lap.

"Today we are doing something different. This is a *couples* coaching session."

Ruby blew out. "Uh, we are not a couple."

"That may be a part of your problem." I pointed to her posters with my braced hand. "Dog has communicated her goals with me. It seems she would like to spend more time with others."

"She *talked* to you?" Ruby's mouth hung open. "She's a guinea pig."

"Just because she doesn't speak doesn't mean we can't listen." I was glad I'd grabbed my best scarf. A strong accessory would get me through this breakthrough session. "When you first brought Dog to me, she squeaked a lot, a sign of distress. The other day, when Logan and I played with her, she purred. Dog doesn't like being alone."

Dog looked up at Ruby and purred in agreement.

This was all obvious to me and to Dog. But not Ruby. And that was something she had to figure out for herself.

"If Dog's goal is to have more companionship, how are you going to accomplish that with her?" I asked.

"So . . . Dog is melancholy because of *me*?" Ruby chewed on her lip. "Because I don't spend enough time with her?"

I held myself back from shouting *AND MAYBE THE*

DOG POSTERS DON'T MAKE HER FEEL TOO HOT, EITHER. "If that's the case, what is the next step?"

"I guess I don't show her that much attention," Ruby said. "I don't know if I told you this, but I wanted a dog, not a guinea pig."

Duh and double duh. "But you don't have a dog."

"Right. I have a guinea pig." Ruby looked around her room. "The problem is, I have to leave her sometimes. I can't always be with her."

"What can you do about that?" I asked.

"Should I give Dog to someone else?"

No! That's not what I wanted. Ugh, this was really difficult. Telling someone what to do was way easier than letting them figure things out for themselves.

I spotted a pet store catalog on Ruby's desk. She'd used it to cut out pictures of dogs for her collage. There was an ad in there that might help. "Can you think of any other solutions?"

Ruby squinted at the paper. "I could . . . buy another guinea pig? So she has a friend?"

Bingo!

Dog purred in Ruby's arms. Ruby looked down at her pet. "She's purring! Wow, that's so cool. You're . . . you're pretty cool, Dog."

The way she looked at Dog this time was different— Ruby didn't look at Dog and wish she was a different animal. Ruby looked at Dog and saw a guinea pig. A guinea pig she wanted to love.

"You're right," she said. "I need to bond with Dog more. And . . . I'll talk to my mom. I don't know how she will feel about another pet, but if they play with each other, it might help Dog with her melancholy. And if not, well, then . . . maybe she goes to live with someone who can give Dog the attention she deserves."

I didn't stick my fist in the air and jump up and down, celebrating my groundbreaking breakthrough. But I wanted to. Hot dog, did I want to. "I'm glad you were both able to achieve your goals."

Dog was still happily purring. I should have brought my camera so I could film her for my infomercial.

"I wish I'd earned that scholarship money." I sighed. "Helping people was fun. Pets, too."

"What do you mean *was*?" Ruby asked. "You're still doing this, aren't you?"

"I don't think so." I picked at a string on my slacks.

"I only did the life coaching thing so I could win the BOO scholarship. My mom's going to sign me up for other activities now. I don't even know if I'll have time. Or gumption."

Ruby grabbed my shoulders. "Willis Wilbur, you look at me."

I looked at her. I'm good at looking at people. Really looking.

"You are a LIFE coach! And setbacks are part of LIFE!" Ruby was pointing at me. I think Dog was, too, but I couldn't really tell. "If you can figure out how to get a dog lover to love her guinea pig named Dog, you can make a business happen. It's your destiny."

There was a very useful skill I'd learned while life coaching. That skill was coming up with the *but* in a bad situation.

But!

I didn't win the scholarship . . . but I had four clients now. And I had that great feeling you get when you try your best. And I knew how to make things happen as my own person. And oh, there were so many other positive parts of this job. Everything I said to the scholarship committee was true.

Life coaching *was* my destiny. Simple as that. Even if I had to go to baseball camp all day, every day, I could still do life coaching in between. First thing in the morning, before I went to bed. Or I could do it in my dreams! I could be the first life coach to visit people while I slept!

"Your advice is more valuable than rubies, Ruby! Thank you."

"Does that mean I get my next session free?" Ruby asked.

I handed her a stress ball. "Nope."

I skipped home.

PRO TIP #12:
Skipping isn't very cool.

But (another *but!*) I didn't care.

CHAPTER 22

The Very Special Person Plate!

As soon as I got home, my mom called me into the kitchen. There was a sandwich on our Very Special Person plate. Did she have a friend coming over?

"Bug, have a seat."

I sat at the head of the table.

"No, in front of your sandwich, silly," Mom said.

"You made me a special sandwich?" I asked. "I told you I *didn't* win the scholarship, right?"

Mom reached over and squeezed my hand. "You don't need to win the scholarship to be a winner, kiddo."

And then my dad came into the room with a plate of sugar cookies! I looked around the room to see if there was a hidden camera somewhere. Maybe Mom and Dad were filming a secret family reality show called *Summer Fun Plan!* and this was all part of their TV series all along?

"We think running a business is a great way to spend your summer," Dad said, smiling. "You handled the situation at your party very well."

"And we already made you that sign and set up an office." Mom shrugged. "It'd be a bummer to let that go to waste."

"Although I wouldn't mind having the garage back," Dad said.

"So . . . I don't have to do scout camp or intense Ping-Pong training this summer?" I asked.

Mom shook her head. "Not unless you are life coaching a Ping-Pong professional. As long as you stay busy with this new job, we're happy to support you."

I bit into my sandwich. The summer was sparkly and open now. I could probably double my business by July. Triple it, even. Then there's the podcast, YouTube series, the merchandising and Willis Wilbur action figure, and—wow, we could create a life coaching movie series. Should I play myself or get Michael Morales?

Logan raced inside the house and grabbed my arm. "You! Phone calls! Clients!"

"What are you saying?" I asked.

Logan gulped in air. "Our phone has been ringing all day. A bunch of business owners want you to coach their kids! And Adrian told the whole mountain biking club that he's meeting with you. You have six appointments next Monday, and five on Tuesday! Willis . . . we're open for business!"

We jumped up and down in a little circle dance. Mom and Dad toasted each other with sugar cookies.

190

I ran to the front door.

Logan followed. "Where are you going?"

"To get a new bow tie. Or maybe a scarf. Or maybe both."

Logan threw up her hands. "Seriously? Right now? We have so much to do!"

"Fashion is high on the list." I skipped down the walkway. "I already wore my two best bow ties to the launch and committee meeting. And I've worn my gray scarf all over town. Can you *imagine* what would happen if I wore the same thing next time my clients see me? Remember this quote from Rachel Zoe: 'Style is a way to say who you are without having to speak.'"

Logan rolled her eyes. She needed to deliver all the surveys to the new clients. And come up with a filing system.

"I'm renegotiating my contract!" Logan called as I zipped away. "I want 85 percent!"

192

THE END

THE WILLIS WILBUR INTERVIEW:

From
GARAGE
OFFICE
to
MILLIONAIRE
MIRACLE
WORKER

195

Instead of listing every celebrity who has worked with life coach Willis Wilbur, we should list all those who haven't. That list is a big fat zero.

Because Willis has worked with everyone who is anyone.

Yet the charismatic, remarkable, talented, funny, flexible, zany, genius, handsome Willis Wilbur doesn't let his fame and fortune stop him from being so likable. Today, Willis greets me in his Malibu home. He's wearing both a scarf and a bow tie (a fashion trend he himself invented) and a very friendly smile. Although I have interviewed countless celebrities and artists for a big-name magazine, I've never been so overwhelmed. I mean, it's Willis Wilbur.

He's like the Beatles of life coaching.

After settling down with some peppermint tea, Willis tells me about the fateful summer at the tender age of nine when he first became a life coach.

"I almost became a decorator, you know." He laughs, his emerald eyes crinkling. "Then I sprained my wrist on this awful coffee table and the rest . . . well, the rest is history."

History indeed. We all know the story of Dog the guinea pig. And Margo Clawson, one of the youngest students ever at Stanford, which I believe is a very important college. And Willis's best friend, Shelley, who plays on the Hawaii softball team. Willis has coached thousands to become the best versions of themselves. He has his own candy line, fragrance line, and of course, there's the Willis Wilbur theme park that opens next summer.

"Now that you're ten," I begin.

"And three-quarters," he adds.

"Of course. Nearly eleven. But now that you're in fifth grade, or you would be in fifth grade if you didn't grad-uate early and get your college degree in two months, do you still have the same goals you had when you first started, so many months ago?"

Willis seems to think about this. I sit in silence, listening to the waves crash against the shore outside his mansion.

"Willis!" It's Logan Wilbur, Willis's little sister. Logan is a success-ful life coach in her own right. She took over the kid coaching branch of the business last year, when Willis reached double digits and could not keep saying no to all the celebrity client requests. "Did you eat all the Girl Scout cookies?"

Willis frowns. "I put the Thin Mints in the freezer."

"You always do that!" Logan moans. "I don't know why you like them frozen. Ugh, now I have to go find some other Girl Scouts to sell me room temperature ones."

"What's it like working alongside your brother?" I ask Logan, who has blue streaks in her hair and a very cool leather jacket.

"Who is this guy?" Logan asks Willis.

"My interviewer," Willis says.

I wave at Logan. She sorta smiles but does not wave back.

"Willis got where he is because he didn't win that scholarship," Logan says. "He worked double hard. By the end of that summer, we had the biggest life coaching business in the county. Remember that, Will? Remember how we had to move out of Mom and Dad's house and into the business park on Main Street?"

Willis nods. "That was one busy summer."

If I ever invent a time machine, I would go two places: First, to see the Beatles in concert, maybe hang out with them before they were famous. The other would be to travel to those early summer days. I could afford to hire Willis as my life coach back then. Now he charges a thousand dollars a minute.

Logan eases next to her brother on the green velvet coach. "Now, if you want to hear a really crazy story, we need to tell you what happened at the end of the summer, right before school started."

Willis groans. "Don't you have some cookies to buy?"

Again, I can't believe I have this opportunity to be in the presence of greatness. I double-check my recorder and settle into the luxurious couch. By the sparkle in Logan's eyes, I can tell that the story of this next adventure is something I don't want to miss . . .

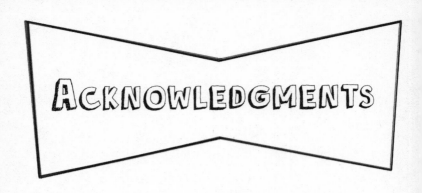

Acknowledgments

If there's one thing I learned in all my life coaching research, it's that authentic praise and recognition are super important. Same with thanking people . . .

First I would like to thank ME—or the me from like two years ago—for discovering this idea and writing the story, because even though it takes a village to publish a book, it mostly takes an author. Also, positive self-talk is important. Way to go, Lindsey!

Matt and Jamie Kirby! For that fateful lunch where we discussed a writing life coach class and then said,

"Wouldn't it be funny if there was a kid life coach?" I called dibs and now here we are. Yay, Matt and Jamie!

Sarah Davies for her many years of working with me as I try many new things. And for mostly getting my sense of humor (and trusting me when you don't). You're the best, Sarah!

Nathaniel Tabachnik for being the most perfect editor for this book. Like if I were creating an editor for Willis's best seller, I would write you (and probably have you hold a shuffleboard stick because you're just that awesome). Your patience and dedication are unparalleled. Everyone cheer for Nathaniel!

Daniel Duncan for bringing Willis to life in all his gumption and glory. All of Willis's friends and family are beautifully drawn, too. You're tops, Daniel!

The rest of the Penguin Workshop team for giving me money to write this book. Oh, and also publishing it. When we make a billion dollars, I will buy us all an island.

203

In fact, you can set up an office there. Way to be team players, Penguin!

Elle Clawson and Sophie Jo Finlayson. Such sharp beta readers. Your feedback was so helpful and astute. I can't wait to read your books someday. Myndie Tullis for life coaching tips. Readers rock!

Lisa Schroeder and Camile Andros for reading early drafts of Willis. Erin Summerill for helping me find Shelley's story. David Gill for insightful, clever revisions. Also, for listening to exactly what I *wanted* at VCFA and then ensuring my experience was precisely what I *needed* instead. Authors are the coolest!

My kids: MacKay, Rylee, Emila, Miles, Talin, and Logan (especially Logan, who is every bit as fun as the Logan in this book). I really love kids and I really love each of you. James: any time I got stumped on Willis, I thought, *What Would James Do?* Your generous optimism and compassion helped frame this book . . . and actually, it's the foundation of our whole life together. Let's hear it for family, folks!

Lastly—YOU! Yes, you holding this best-selling, award-winning, life-changing book in your hands. As Christopher Robin once said to Winnie-the-Pooh, "You are braver than you believe, and stronger than you seem, and smarter than you think."

The world is your oyster, kid (or your shell)!

—Lindsey Leavitt

Photo © Erin Summerill

Lindsey Leavitt is the author of loads of extra funny books for kids, tweens, and teens. You should read them, right away, before she starts a podcast, a reality show, or life coaching empire (she would do an Authors and Their Dogs series, but her schnoodle tends to steal the spotlight). Visit her online at www.lindseyleavitt.com.